Readopolis

READOPOLIS

Bertrand Laverdure
translated by Oana Avasilichioaei

BookThug
Toronto, 2017
Literature in Translation Series

SECOND PRINTING

Published originally under the title: *Lectodôme* © Bertrand Laverdure &
Le Quartanier, Montreal 2008

English translation copyright © 2017 Oana Avasilichioaei

The production of this book was made possible through the generous assistance
of the Canada Council for the Arts and the Ontario Arts Council. BookThug also
acknowledges the support of the Government of Canada through the Canada Book
Fund and the Government of Ontario through the Ontario Book Publishing Tax
Credit and the Ontario Book Fund.

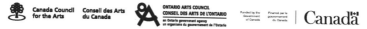

We acknowledge the financial support of the Government of Canada through the
National Translation Program for Book Publishing, an initiative of the *Roadmap
for Canada's Official Languages 2013–2018: Education, Immigration, Communities*, for our
translation activities.

LIBRARY AND ARCHIVES CANADA CATALOGUING IN PUBLICATION

Laverdure, Bertrand, 1967–
[Lectodôme. English]
    Readopolis / Bertrand Laverdure; Oana Avasilichioaei, translator.
—First English edition.

(Literature in translation series)
Translation of: Lectodôme.

Issued in print and electronic formats.
softcover: ISBN 978-1-77166-298-7
html: ISBN 978-1-77166-299-4
pdf: ISBN 978-1-77166-300-7
kindle: ISBN 978-1-771663-01-4

I. Avasilichioaei, Oana, translator II. Title. III. Title: Lectodôme.
English IV. Series: Literature in translation series

PS8573.A815L4213 2017   C843'.54   C2017-900742-4   C2017-900743-2

PRINTED IN CANADA

In memory of Thomas Braichet
(1977–2008)

He who is born today is meant for a much more intensely intellectual life than he who was born a hundred thousand years ago; and yet, notwithstanding the intensity of his individual life, his intelligence will be found to be, so to speak, much more socialized; precisely because of its being so much richer, it will possess much less for itself alone. It is the same with sensibility.

—JEAN-MARIE GUYAU, *A Sketch of Morality Independent of Obligation or Sanction*, translated by Gertrude Kapteyn

Where shall I find the time to do all this non-reading?

—KARL KRAUS, *Half-Truths & One-and-a-Half Truths: Selected Aphorisms*, translated by Harry Zohn

Contents

I.

THE FOUR ACES

I'M RESTING. Dozing off. Doing nothing, just resting. All I want is to lie in bed, arms out like a cross, left cheek on the pillow, legs and chest flat on the mattress. I haven't read anything today and won't read anything before one in the afternoon. I am a reader—what publishing houses call "a member of the editorial board."

Yet there is no editorial board, no summit meeting, no secret gathering to formulate impartial, obvious decisions, ones that are democratic and positive. I am a reader because I have my own view of literature: what it should be; what buttons to sew on a novel's sleeves; what zippers to place throughout a narrative; the ideal length of writers' detestable pipe dreams.

My plight is to rule over the ghosts haunting the world of letters. Deep down, I will always be Hercules standing before the Augean Stables. I devote myself to a soldier's anonymous life. I am sent to the front of others' words, the unbearable, lachrymose bundles of Monsieur Patenaude and Madame Lefebre, Monsieur Hogarteen and Madame Willoska. The unbelievable heap of manuscripts pollutes my consciousness.

Who wouldn't slam into the first wall they see, having realized the sheer madness of human beings, their disrespectful desire to impose all their misfortunes and opinions on us? If it were up to me, I would decree a law against abominable books.

In fact, I abhor all these smooth talkers, these idolaters of the freedom of expression. Okay fine, I get it, people need to express themselves, rejoice, appease their egos, pour out their bitterness, recount their troubles, but then they get it into their heads to publish this Mother of Vinegar, this thick syrup—no, I say! Asinine nonsense. Kill off the whole lot of blowhards, wipe these battalions of human expression off the face of the earth.

I'm resting.

I won't say that I recant, lose my head, sometimes have regrets. But I'm weary, I feel my calm slipping away.

I read because others' torments are part of my labour. I read because the harshest truths and the most ordinary dramas—not to mention extravagant desires—emerge between the clumsy lines of the worst fictions.

Authenticity rests in the clumsiness of writers.

I move only because the earth is round. I lose my temper

only because talent is everywhere; it is spherical, omnipotent, unstoppable, flimsy, murky.

What do we learn from reading a good book, a book that affects and moves us?

What do we learn, exactly? How does this experience enrich us, help us transcend our daily worries?

Books are archives of our restlessness. We live in the era of *Pax Americana*, a unidirectional democracy imposed as a universal cure. We will use banal terms to write about it in studies read by beings with laser-corrected myopia. We will introduce nuances, avoid making generalizations and cookie-cutter judgments, reductive pronouncements. But we will reach the same conclusion: violence rules the world.

I've been a member of an editorial board for almost six years. I read and read and read, convincing myself that this is a natural extension of my scholarly abilities.

For now, my fridge is half empty, but my determination remains intact.

Because I want to be a knight of nihilism, someone withdrawn from the world, I found a lousy second job that lets me feel sorry for myself.

Three days a week, I work in a Couche-Tard convenience store, so I can honour my obligations as tenant and my small pleasures as cultural consumer.

I am an ideologue, and literature suits this shortcoming perfectly. Literature feeds it and encourages it, disseminates it and indulges it.

* * *

Every reader has an inner commentator who is thrilled to decipher like some fragile material the void that stands between the reader and the words. Champollion is the grandmaster of readers, the admiral.

We erroneously give readers of publishing houses a key role. Honestly, defending this rumour only promotes misinformation.

Language is a code, and literature uses the cogwheels of this code to shape the space-time that choreographs humankind. The first inventors of language are writers, then come the stylists and historians.

Literature, that same old tune, that scuffed and ancient leather bag, still exists, and it is never more present than among its enemies: human indifference, ignorance, and laziness.

I live at 3270 Sherbrooke Street East, apartment 4. I don't read without taking breaks.

Walking is my second vocation. I walk north, south, northeast, southeast, northwest, southwest.

What I seek is a sense of continuity, the effect of a long take. A successful walk is one where I become a spectator, a spy.

My penchant for spying leads me to notice commemorative plaques, posters, torn paper stuck to poles, abandoned newspapers, and recycling bins overflowing with sullied books, pages filled with words.

This tablet commemorates those in the service
of the Canadian Pacific Railway Company who,
at the call of the king and the country,
endured hardship, faced danger and finally
passed out of sight of men by the path of duty
and self-sacrifice, giving up their own lives

that others might live in freedom,
let those who come after see to it
that their names be not forgotten

Right next to the former Angus Shops, a brass plaque is affixed to the brick building that now houses CECI (Centre for International Studies and Cooperation). The plaque, more like a bas-relief sculpture, depicts tanks, battleships, planes and cannons, elongated through the effect of perspective, accompanied by cavalry and infantry, captains and commanders. The plaque honours the memory of the CPR workers who lost their lives in World War I.

This plaque is a book. It contains the key lessons we should take from life.

Its presence is no longer noticed; no one stops to contemplate its message. Yet, in just a few lines, we can already read the non-existence of the French-Canadian CPR workers who gave up their innocence for the nation. There's not one French word on the plaque. A unilingual English memorandum, fiercely royalist. The law of economics applied then and still applies now. There is no imperialist grandeur without omission.

This passage now: "endured hardship, faced danger and finally / passed out of sight of men by the path of duty / and self-sacrifice."

Does this not sum up what it means to live among humans?

Now forget a writer's intuition. These lines transcend the brute toil of soldiers, the terse mechanics of orders.

But what exactly do we know about the path of duty and self-sacrifice? We know that it leads to the frontier that conceals us from the sight of others.

If I do not see you, do you still exist?

I was there to catch others' looks, to telescope their field of vision. I surveyed life with appropriate glasses, offering others their tickets to presence. Over time, I started taking notes of the inscriptions I found on my walks, collecting the torn bits of newspaper, trampled brochures, or letters abandoned in the wet grass.

Every morning comes with its harvest of words. Easy pickings every time.

Today, I came home with an entire plaque, a text commemorating the men who sacrificed themselves for the nation.

These spoils were enough.

* * *

Four manuscripts await me on the table.

I ignore them.

The main joy of reading is being idle. We listen to music with no purpose in mind. We occupy time.

Manuscripts are bottles dropped from a sinking ship. They are patient entities.

Authors are definitely not.

Sometimes, the naïveté is touching. Someone in Saint-Rémi or the Town of Mount Royal is waiting. They wait for me. They know that public proceedings have been initiated. Having received their acknowledgement letter, they wait. Solitary or sociable, indifferent or sick, they wait. I listen to their heartbeat, pick up a page, read one line, casually leaf through the manuscript. I look over the cover letter. Read three pages in the middle and two from the end.

The publishing house gives me two weeks to read four manuscripts, assigning me a quota of pages, always the same, based on what I can do, never more than 150,000 words. A normal human being who lives to the age of eighty-four, well trained, with sound command of the French language and average curiosity, represents approximately 42,000 pages of confessions and diaries. If everyone in the world were to become literate, most tree species would go extinct.

If it were as easy to educate as it is to subjugate, we would have less difficulty imposing goodwill.

I am not particularly keen on reading for the nth time a botched historical novel or a detestable true story dripping with so many of the usual homilies that it doesn't hold water.

I've lost count of the horror stories or self-help books, the memoirs and fantastical ravings. Don't take me for a cynic. A novel has no good subject per se. Everything is allowed, everything is acceptable. Let's say it's more a matter of vocation, general knowledge, and practice. In a few paragraphs, I can identify the ignorant and the deranged, the diligent and the dedicated. Everyone has written at least one poem or short story in their life.

Despite my irritation, I believe it's important to take the time to congratulate every person who has completed one or several short stories, a novel, or an essay. Regardless of what happens to these manuscripts, a sensitive explorer stands before you. Don't mock him. Through a curious effect of perspective, he is more alive than you. He is an unveiler, and he has you at gunpoint. He will leave a testament more honest than any notarized inheritance. At worst, he is a feeble fool, at best, an agitated witness, perhaps even a writer.

* * *

Yesterday afternoon, I went to the Marie-Reine-du-Monde Cathedral. As I said, I like to be idle, to stroll. Reading is a profession marked by pauses. Please be patient.

I use the period, the colon, the comma. I have only three friends who are not put off by my profound desire for solitude: Pascal, Courrège, and Maldonne. Pascal refuses to have anything to do with me, Courrège still writes from time to time, and Maldonne hasn't talked to me since I put a stop to our sexual relations.

Two or three times a week, I feel the need to speak and hear a response, to touch the people I know, to become an empty glass that is filled by the water of the world.

Yesterday, I didn't feel this urgent need. I was completely alone. I had been reading Perec's *Je suis né*, and Georges had infected me with his asceticism, his diligent passion for solitude.

I drift in and out of books, and respect the state in which they leave me. It's not that I am impressionable. After all, I am a reader by profession. I get paid to assess the real and the sustaining. I accept that books change me, but I don't impose the same on you. To each their disposition, to each their innocence and function. In thirty-four years of reading, I have never tried to ascertain my colleagues' level of engagement or to make sure that the book had been read, the material understood. Much freer than a film spectator, less constrained, technologically speaking, than a web user, the reader is first and foremost a connoisseur of the tactile, a sensualist and artist, a master of slowness. The reader's workforce is made up of contemplation, photocopying (like photosynthesis for plants), the length, heft and shedding of complexity's leaves.

So I was alone on the steps of the cathedral. The guide's tiny office was deserted. Only an elderly woman stood smoking nearby. I didn't make the sign of the cross, and it fitted the mood. Georges Delfosse had painted all the wall paintings adorning the cathedral. Another era spoke to me. Reading the same book several times over alters our state. Especially if it's a self-help book, a contemplative poetry collection, a fantasy novel that interprets a way of life. I understand them much more than they think I do. I am one of them. I believe in them.

I looked for a brochure and found one. There was no guide; the brochure would do.

* * *

The Couche-Tard next to the Joliette subway stop, my evening job. It's not quite right to say that it's adjacent to it; I always had the impression that it was embedded in the subway stop, joined to it by an imperceptible connective tissue.

A chrome yellow glow, yellow bricks, harsh lighting. These were my surroundings.

With the usual discomfort, I had donned the large Town & Country navy-blue shirt, made in Canada, 65% polyester and 35% cotton. The stylized Vittorio Fiorucci owl, a winking red bird, hovered above the store's name embroidered on the shirt. The whole ensemble was supposed to reassure customers of my good intentions and professionalism. Or in any case, lend me the authority to serve them.

A circus beast, like all logo beasts, the winking red owl didn't threaten anyone. It instilled a kind of complicit relationship that I would develop with the customers of the convenience store. I was complicit in their cravings, malnourishment, fleeting pleasures, their poverty, rage, and small obsessions.

In the 1970s, the Office québécois de la langue française, the province's very own version of the Académie française, was dismayed by the multitude of words used to describe the corner store—including anglicisms such as *magasin d'accommodation*, from "accommodation store".... So the Office recommended that the term *dépanneur* be used instead. Unlike similar attempts in France (in 1987, the French government promoted the term *bazarette*, but it never caught on), *dépanneur* quickly integrated itself into the local parlance of both languages, bridging the widening cultural divide of the time. English-speaking Montrealers are the only Canadians who buy beer at "the dep."

From an article by Christopher DeWolf, published in *Maisonneuve* 7, February 2004, p. 12–13.

Why has this type of store prospered to such an extent? Why has it infiltrated our lives, our literature, overrun our urban environments? In Montreal, there are more deps than mail boxes!

I'll try to explain. In the early sixties, the distribution systems of soft drink companies and food conglomerates surged. Shopping malls grew like mushrooms in fields everywhere, became warehouses, dispersed wherever the taxpayers—the middle class—lived. In poorer neighbourhoods and even in more affluent ones, it was undoubtedly judged that being too far from these food service centres hindered modern procurement, a life now governed and fed by a pleasant prosperity.

In an epoch when stores were closed on Sundays in Quebec and were not open twenty-four hours, most people developed the need to acquire their comfort foods, basic necessities, cigarettes, beer, and soft drinks within walking distance from their homes. The shopping mall was devised in relation to the car, its ability to transport things over long distances, and the oil companies that were overjoyed by this windfall. In contrast, the convenience store was devised for walkers.

Shopping mall = driving a car

Convenience store = walking

In accordance with market logic, deps reproduced the sales systems of shopping malls, but on a smaller scale. The owners of these new SMEs had understood that they needed to offer their walking customers the best-selling foodstuffs, the canned goods that were in fashion, and everything that would please the kids, most of whom were initiated into their first monetary exchanges in these small shopping schools. In supermarkets, it was necessary to create bagging stations and offer home delivery. In convenience stores, people only bought a few products at a time, so baggers lost their usefulness, yet owners quickly gave in to the temptation to imitate the delivery service of supermarkets.

Most supermarkets were first established in these small commercial villages set up along highways. The concept of the supermarket permanently united retail trade and food distribution. An oil- and car-driven world, a disposable world.

A world in which a packaged chicken has an expiration date, as does a shirt at Zellers (since fashion follows the cycle of the seasons).

Everything for sale is perishable because the absolute is not commercial.

In some cases, we find comfort in the perishable because it resembles the absolute. We'll always find cans of Campbell's Cream of Mushroom soup on the shelves; in most Zellers, Glad garbage bags, Vim cleaning products, J Cloths, Ajax and bath towels, Drano, La Parisienne bleach, and Spic and Span. The world of home cleaning and food storage rightly fights, by any means possible, against the endless onslaught of decline, clutter, and dust. A benevolent coating to appease our commonplace interiors, our accustomed stomachs, and our fantasy of imperishable food. I protect my life against stains and refuse. I fight for a clean conscience. I am North American to the core.

Refuse is the beginning of death; the eternal preservation of food, one of our Edenic dreams.

*　*　*

More pathetic messages from Maldonne.

She is fond of me. Sad euphemism. Three messages in my voicemail. I thought I would be seeing *Love on the Run* for the third time, but instead the revenants of *Hour of the Wolf* are hounding me.

I am living in a Bergman film.

Madness is a banal theme in literature. Like every good reader, I have fed on its mysteries and crises more than once. In fact, when the character of the painter's wife, played by

Liv Ullmann in *Hour of the Wolf*, asks her husband if, in accordance with the curious logic of sharing that governs a couple's life, his painting delirium will haunt her one day, will grow on her like the roots of a weed, her naïveté is not meant to be laughable. This simple woman, who has fallen in love with a great artist, nevertheless asks herself a good question: Doesn't a couple actually resemble a machine of mutual cloning in a way? Imperceptibly, the gaps close up and scar, the mindsets merge.

We continuously secrete words that annihilate anything outside the confines of the union between two people. On the surface, it all happens through the regime of words, but inside this flow of words, the flow of hormones feeds on the reactive energy aroused in the encounter between two individuals. The mandate of these two cells is to merge into one. In short, everything should be transmitted, everything keeps reacting and adapting forever.

Madness, therefore, is transmissible. But up to what point?

Maldonne became infatuated with me after one night of dissipation. Ordinary evening, usual urban scenario. Drinks in some bar, an invite to a party at Pascal's, the earnest end-of-the-night search for the nearest 24-hour resto, an Italian poutine, and my arm over her shoulder, the hesitations before saying our goodbyes, my body automatically pressing against hers, then some random phrase, always meaningless, slipping through her lips.

I woke up the next morning: splitting headache, stiff all over, the usual feelings of regret flitting through my mind, and a faint sense of well-being enveloping me. Trying to recover.

MALDONNE: You okay? Not dreaming too much?

GHISLAIN (*laboriously*): What do you prescribe, if I can't go on?

MALDONNE (*getting closer, kissing him*): You know what I would like right now...

A bit of vaudeville perfectly suits the morning games of lovers. Sexuality is the stage for a wide variety of gibes, which, according to the models imagined by the screenwriters of the sixties, live on in daily life in simplified forms.

With Maldonne, I don't remember feeling anything other than an unbearable desire to perform. We dramatized everything. From mornings to nights out, from lovemaking to our social life. A few months of this medicine were enough to thoroughly irritate me, not because this improvised tension annoyed me; on the contrary, rather she was seriously starting to wear me down. Her passion continued to grow, was even roused by my hesitation, my doubts, while I gradually lost all my resources, all my motivation.

I became sullen, and she refused to see it.

She knocked on my door at all hours. She inundated me with emails, pulverized all records of the number of telephone calls.

Surreptitiously, I was forced to reduce our interactions to recreational sex.

The ridiculousness of my convictions at the time saddens me all the more because I was sure that our pact would draw on unsuspected resources in the other. I was so naive.

She rebelled, knew how to circumvent my defences. She wore me down.

The sirens sang. I stuffed my ears with earplugs. Calm returned. Every time I would pull out the orange cones from my ear canals, the sirens would redouble their ardour, devising new odes in the dead of night.

*   *   *

Reading is a civic act.

True autodidacts are privileged citizens.

I make no claim to being one of them. I am a reader of novels and essays, poetry and news articles.

My abilities as a reader do not go beyond that. However, I know determined readers, avid autodidacts who only really need one book, one instruction manual to grasp everything, absorb everything, set everything in motion. First and foremost, autodidacts are intelligent people. They constitute a category of readers for whom books are doors onto the world, telltale signs.

My books do not hold all the answers. For me, they're the source of anarchic individuality, of intellectual musings on the world.

Fans of how-to books do not come from the same family of readers. We don't speak the same language. Our libraries are nothing alike. We don't visit the same historic sites. They will prefer the labs of inventors, residencies of politicians, sites of decisive battles, whereas I will choose the houses of writers, their living rooms and bedrooms.

Readers of results, readers of impressions. People always stand on one side or the other of a divide.

The first category includes all readers of history and practical how-to books. They appreciate details, technical accuracy, applied theories. For them, reading is a civic act because it helps them assimilate more and more information about their environment. They are encyclopaedists without knowing it. Readers of impressions are part of another tribe—one of emotionalists and philosophers. For them, the world is a magical, wide-open book, a never-ending fairy tale, a universe of eclectic and complex individuals. For this type of reader, devouring a novel or carefully reading a collection of poetry becomes a civic act.

Here is what, for me, makes a book: an individual's artistic ability to grasp all the nuances of their affiliation with the real world—the physical world, the mental world—and their power to transcend theses nuances.

Since its connection to reality is more immediate, the tribe of practicalists tends to regard the reading program of the impressionists as a trivial pastime. I am aware of this, but don't take it seriously.

In the concept of the world that is particular to practicalists, a will to act in reality serves as a *modus vivendi*. If you do not think in this way, you're ranked below those who watch soaps on TV.

Whereas for the impressionists, reading is an end in itself, a civilizing act, a philosophical-aesthetic experience that is satisfying on its own, fully complete as such. To add the finishing touches to the picture, we would need to speak of experiential patience and truth.

The reader of novels seeks a means to delve into the world, to grasp all the subtle connections between individuals, to gather fine and sometimes exceedingly allusive impressions about the movements of beings. The reader of novels and poetry is also interested in the workings of the vocal apparatus and the creative achievements of language. Ethically inclined, this reader does not overlook the animals and plants responding in their anthropomorphic idioms, which the reader enjoys translating. The practical reader calls this childishness, but the impressionistic reader retorts that to imagine the existence of a Dr. Dolittle and sympathize absurdly with the suffering of animals, thanks to a character born of the imagination, offers a kind of comic relief and lessens the angst of not being able to fully communicate with their quadruped or hexapod friends. The impressionistic reader knows full well that we nurture the imagination through imagination.

As everyone can probably guess, I belong to the category of impressionistic readers, and I am no worse off for it.

My friend Pascal, on the other hand, belongs to the category of practical readers, autodidacts that take a somewhat cynical view towards those in my category. I never get out of it easily. I've never been at ease with placid friends.

* * *

I eat poorly, then hurry to the movies to watch fluff, serenades, and shams. The passivity and stupor of the spectator suits me just fine. In general, because I read such dreary manuscripts about all the problems of living in society, I have developed a therapeutic response to this intellectual chore, namely watching mainstream cinema, achieving catharsis through pure entertainment.

Reading is work. Too many intelligent and sophisticated books exist. I feel a deep shame if I comply with the marketing and buzz of the moment. I don't have this devotion for the cinema. The book is another matter.

I don't dare entertain myself by reading. It's not out of

snobbery; only a show of respect towards an activity that teaches us to live fully and to think. I belong to the cult of the devotees of the book.

However, I'm not a creepy type. What I'm talking about is more like the game "Simon Says," in which one of the players, in this case me, refuses to follow the rules, yet keeps observing the game. I withdraw from the world. I accept my role as observer, an inactive pedestrian in a constant state of meditation before what he sees, what he reads. This is not quite a spiritual phase, the last step towards philosophical and personal wisdom, as Kierkegaard saw it. Nor does it fall within an aesthetic phase, if we follow the same track. Rather, it's something between the two.

I would call this state the reading phase.

The reading phase propels us into the world of *readopolis*. And the readopolis produces a complex state of concentration that enables us, by decoding a series of written or printed letters, to reproduce at will the sense of being detached from the world, the impression of doing precision work on a fragile object placed before us. The sentence that you are currently reading, the words that you are more or less quickly deciphering, your eyes that have already scanned this progression of commas are therefore functioning in readopolis mode.

Incidentally, reading is my work and, as with any profession, we come to indentify with a model that the stereotypes connected to our position convey. For me, reading has become a kind of ritual of existence. I am obsessed with practising this art form—as it is one.

I got **READOPOLIS** printed in orange Cooper Black font on a dark green, cotton T-shirt. I had a worshipping fit, and I'm not sorry about it. A fetishist and pathetic occupation; I accept it.

The book is an auspicious gateway to the multitude, to diversity, to the most disparate forms of knowledge and sensibilities. I've always been certain of this. By reading for publishers, writing reader's reports, notes, comments, critical remarks in the margins of manuscripts, I penetrated this truth. I lived it day in and day out at the time. I had attained the reading phase. I accessed the readopolis mode at will.

My ascension to the reading phase had increased my critical faculties tenfold. I bore the onus of acceptance or rejection increasingly well.

I was surrounded by nonprofessional readers, my friends, often more cultured than me, but I had become a reader who, for his part, could lay claim to his professionalism.

In other words, I now read to earn money.

It was real work, therefore, this sacrifice that brings us, like any sacrifice, to the screen behind which humanity no longer sees us.

*   *   *

Maldonne was a fan, a total fanatic, of Hubert Aquin. She had managed to ferret out a signed copy of *Prochain épisode** in a used bookstore on Laurier Avenue. She didn't flinch when the bookseller asked $100 for it. Like every dedicated junkie of bookshops and booksellers, she knew that signed Hubert Aquins were hard to find. He was a drinker, a car

---

* Aquin's 1965 classic novel, *Prochain épisode*, was translated by Sheila Fischman and published in 2001 as *Next Episode* by New Canadian Library. (Trans.)

racing and sex fanatic, but, it seems, parsimonious with his signature.

Supply and demand in the world of sellers of signed books was an inexact science, a mysterious gothic tale.

No statistics or directories of signed books existed that could have interested the hordes of aficionados. No register could guarantee us that we were not dealing with a fake, that the author didn't sign books compulsively, or that the rarity of the book or signature of a particular writer was well and truly real.

The world of used bookstores and dealers of rare and out-of-print books worked in impenetrable, ghostly, mysterious ways. You first needed to join this brotherhood of yellowed paper.

Maldonne and I were members of this club. Our expression of faith had been duly noted in multiple FileMaker, Access, and other management software files of these high priests of books.

François Côté and Abe knew us. The pallid coots of the Chercheur de trésors bookstore knew us, and the others— bearded, catted, bespectacled or lacking personal hygiene and greasy-haired—had noticed us. Some knew our names, if not our tastes.

We were part of a family. We too were treasure seekers.

* * *

Of my friends, Courrège is by far the most polite and at the same time, the most demonstrative. She works at the Grande Bibliothèque.

She can often be found on the second floor (although the employees of the main library are caught in a human cycle of perpetual relocation so as to never get bored at work). This floor is dedicated to literature. On neatly arranged shelves, Quebec literature has been distributed among other national literatures. In French translation, of course. No fear of a socioeconomic ghetto here; we have been placed into the world with no fuss. To see Marie-Claire Blais so close to Beckett gives us an intense feverish hope, but also reassures us of the legitimacy of our cultural expectations. We carried some weight; we had a place to fill. If there had been a cultural Olympics, we would have qualified.

Is this just wishful thinking? Possibly. The fact remains that living in an urban area, you need to read. So the battle is already partly won.

My friends and I were trying to increase the rate of quality reading. Courrège, who was named after a perfume and didn't care—an androgynous beauty laughing at her own physical anonymity that hid and stripped her of sex appeal—had the ability, rare among readers, to see reality from its less disappointing angles. Courrège was an optimistic reader. A rare case. Her engagement and enthusiasm nourished me. For me, she was a messenger of intelligence, a diligent of the stock of convictions that fluctuate with the times and the fatalistic commentaries of media-savvy intellectuals.

I envied her high spirits, which never verged on exaltation.

A nice character, she was also a fan of game shows. She dreamed of knowing everything and was fascinated by the propensity of television game shows to reward a participant who had the knowledge required to answer two dozen questions over the course of one show.

Culture could give us returns. Culture was worth its weight in gold. Culture deserved our attention. Culture also had its athletes.

Tapping her index finger on the counter, she had frequently told us about these athletes, these outstanding memorizers that gratified the television networks. Courrège was one of these contestants. Not the best one of all, or the most dispassionate, but insightful enough to often qualify and be part of the 13% of people who know, people who respond, people who work their memory for the benefit of those who need it.

I don't know if Courrège really was more cultured than my other friends.

Than Pascal, for example, who never seemed to be caught off guard in a conversation, who always quoted the right authors and was seldom wrong about the references one must list if one wishes to prove equal to an expert in a conversation.

Maldonne knew everything there was to know about Hubert Aquin and a few other filmmakers and authors. To enter into her areas of interest meant admitting our ignorance and cursory knowledge.

Courrège was more restless, eager to ask questions, to retain it all. She had the personality of the eternal student. Never completely confident in how much she knew, but also never second-rate or ridiculous, either. She recorded information, classified and compiled it, organized it according to systems of organic, logical steps. Her epistemological metabolism worked perfectly.

Less keen on calling than on emailing, Courrège emailed me two or three times a week. She took advantage of our friendship to inflict the saga of her private life on me—her attempts at seduction and her successes.

I. THE FOUR ACES

So yesterday, when I opened her *n*th email, I learned that she had participated in the pilot for a game show on Télé-Québec.

* * *

To: readmeagain@sympatico.ca
From: earnestoearnesto@gmail.com

Hey Ghis!

You'll never believe it! I'm full of love for everyone, I tell you, full of love! Feel like running in the fields, the forests, the streets! I've got to reread Queneau!

They picked me, Ghis! Last Sunday, I participated in the pilot for a Télé-Québec quiz show. Kind of like *Reach for the Top*, but in teams of three and with the right to consult your team. *Facile!* A friend from Quebec City had sent me the info, knowing my quick-response symptoms... So I signed up on the game's website, the *Tournoi des mètres*, and after completing a round of three games, I qualified!

General knowledge is not some dead weight, it's sparring material!

This is the first time in my life that I set foot in Télé-Québec! I was summoned at 8 am at 1000 Fullum St. End of the road, just before you hit the river... the building, a huge drab cube, kind of squashed under the bridge... inside is where it gets interesting. At the entrance, you walk on tiles, a strange black mosaic with a long blue stripe. At reception, I wrote my name in the register, the whole time eyeballing the large mosaic scarred by the long blue line... looking at it a bit closer, following the line of colour against the dark background, I realized that the names of Quebec towns were stuck to the blue strip, made of thousands of tesserae, blue, brown, yellow and white tiles carefully cut by the artist. I felt so dumb not understanding what I was walking on. It wasn't until the first break... as soon as the floor manager brought us juice, zucchini bread, coffee and glasses on a trolley... I'm such an idiot... it's so obvious, so obvious, I suddenly got it: we were walking on the Saint Lawrence River! A large mosaic of the Saint Lawrence River with the towns that stretch along it and criss-cross it... I think you've got to visit Télé-Québec just to have a look at the floor in the entryway...

I was there to test the hosts... This was the task of our small group, the six of us who had qualified... Only two women in the lot... Unpopular guys seem to have this pathetic mania for becoming game show contestants at any cost...

As for the studio... cables, cameras and computers, a nervous director... The set amounted to two cable cars, a garish red one and a Joliette-subway-yellow one. Ever seen the Joliette subway stop? Just kidding... It's always surprising to be on a TV set. The fake decor, trashy imitation, the wires, the gummed tape, the nails, the small Xs on the floor of the contestant's booth... The whole theatrical side, the smell backstage, the feverish state of fellow contestants... Everything seems to stem from fortuitous joy, a world out of the ordinary, a universe of artifice ruled by precise Darwinian laws:

only beautiful people, only individuals able to improvise with elegance, or with controlled vulgarity, only faces that look good onscreen...

With my black dress and glasses, I looked exactly like the stereotypical intellectual... an intellectual who had escaped from Saint-Germain-des-Prés in 1948. By strange coincidence, the three members of my team (they paired us up) all wore some black. My teammate with an athlete's body and bearing reminded me of an SS youth on probation from a boot camp for young delinquents... I quickly started to rely on him, he knew all the answers... Pressing the button that stopped the ticking of the seconds... Not moving a muscle, hardly cracking a smile... He was a rock... Imperturbable, everything that came out of his mouth was fair, considered, right... (And by the way, Stéphane E. Roy (the ridiculous accountant on *Caméra Café* on TVA) totally botched up his audition for the host. Nervous, badly prepared and with bad hair, he made jokes that fell flat and seemed to be struggling with his own frustration at not being able to answer all the questions himself... In short, he seemed overwhelmed. Besides failing his part, he couldn't manage to follow how the game was unfolding... A total disaster.) I learned later, cuz we had time to socialize a bit between the takes, that Jean-Marc, the SS champ, was a radiology intern at Notre-Dame Hospital... scrupulously elitist. In fact, he was the only contestant to ask the "content editor" (that's the job title; in the world of books, we call this the writer) when the episodes of the show would start being filmed. He already saw himself there, confident, a trooper... but never looking to provoke, to swagger... a professional contestant selected by the Darwinian laws of television.

I don't think I embarrassed anyone... I was wrong two or three times, put my foot in my mouth suggesting wrong answers to my teammates... We lost two games out of three... Looking back, I guess I did embarrass myself a few times.

What is the name of the village bard in Asterix?

One of my co-contestants quickly whispered to the leader: *Cacofonix*... Nervous, my nerves fried, knowing that our score was falling behind the other team's, I panicked, said with steadfast conviction to Pierre-Luc, the guy in the lead: *Getafix*... I shrieked *Getafix* in his ear... He, also nervous, trusting me (the certainty with which I passed him the answer had undoubtedly convinced him), hit the red hot button in front of him and spat out: *Getafix!*

Clang! Suddenly a blue cable car appeared on our screen, unhooked from the cable, tilted over and dropped into the void. *Boinnnnnnng!* Wrong answer...

Wrong answer... The sound effect was ridiculous. All that to make us feel guilty, embarrassed... Getafix is the druid, come on, the village druid, the druid, wake up! Bloody hell!

We have to say that we're having fun. Shouldn't get too ambitious, it's only a game... only a game... It's only a game if we want to believe that no one is judging anyone... Ghislain, we have to admit that we're ridiculous at all times because we're afraid to live completely, to live out our pleasures until we exhaust them, until we open the door to excess.

I. THE FOUR ACES

Télé-Québec is going to send me a cheque for $50 to compensate me for the damage inflicted on my small dignity.

I'll take you out to a movie as soon as I get it.

Courrège
xx

2.

THE GOSPEL OF DISTRIBUTION

UNBEARABLE! SHIT, IT'S UNBEARABLE! PEOPLE DON'T reread what they write. It's awful.

Impossible to keep reading this mess. It's beyond my control. I feel like pitching the manuscript out the window. Unbearable.

Twenty pages are plenty. Twenty pages is all it takes, my work is done. I won't go any further. It would drain the last of my remaining strength. But they must be stopped, these keyboard delinquents!

Why am I not a person of private means? I depend on this ecosystem of sorting, an editorial structure based on choices; it's wretched. I go prospecting, shake my little gold pan, throw back the lumps of sand and pebbles. A cat-and-mouse game, a game of promises and rejection letters. Pessoa was convinced that we are slaves, no matter what we undertake, no matter what we do. Revering freedom as we do negatively reveals our utter confusion.

* * *

I earned my thirty dollars—the amount recommended by UNEQ (Union of Quebec Writers). Thirty dollars to read one manuscript. Yet it is not really work; it's a vocation, a calling. But that's the book business, no way around it: everything is meagre, rationed. I'm forced to admit that in some publishing houses, all we're offered is water. I can still see the poor publisher telling me that he is ready to add another member to his reading committee. Then he offers me a glass of water. Pours some warm "Our Compliments" water into a scratched Arcoroc glass. I take it. He will not be giving me my thirty dollars per manuscript. I will be the good prince. Offer him the beggar's deal: four free manuscripts.

It's an obsession. Why do I keep knocking on the doors of publishers who are puny, stingy and broke (hence their stinginess, it's not just for dramatic effect), fishing for work that is only symbolically remunerated? I'm stubborn. I want to be able to say to people that I "work in my field." People feel less sorry for me when I tell them: "I'm not rich, but at least I work in my field." This satisfies them. They're content. They can then tell themselves that no one studies for nothing, that it all leads to employment, that jobs exist to compensate anyone who has completed years of studies, that life is one vast puzzle into which we fit without a hitch, without having to trim the edges, build up the energy, constantly change direction. It's a dream of order. We satisfy our dream of order, a fantasy of social tidiness.

Most people think that society resembles a messy house where we must engage in the household tasks of dusting, scrubbing, clearing out, holding garage sales all year long. When we tell them that we work in our field, we feel as though we're giving them proof that confirms their vision.

I studied in such-and-such field, I work in the same field and there you go, everything is neat and tidy: the underwear in the right drawer, the broom in the closet, the pants in the lower drawer, the coats on their hangers, the dirty clothes in the laundry basket, the living room clean, the furniture dusted. And the bathroom exuding a chemical lemon scent.

The national dream is to fulfil these fantasies countrywide. The management of this flow into appropriate social containers falls upon economists, counsellors, technocrats, journalists, legislators, and politicians.

But it never works.

Desire and utility don't go hand in hand.

It would be so simple to determine the number of candidates needed in every field every year, adjust the enrolment quotas in universities and vocational programs, and carry out a kind of natural selection process in order to keep the unemployment rate as low as possible. But these simplistic principles are pure hallucinations. Nothing is more unpredictable than an individual filled with desire. It's miserable, but we can choose to be poor, not work, change our minds, travel, miss the boat, set off on an adventure, forget our dreams, tempt fate. It's human nature. Since the traditional nuclear family with two kids is no longer imposed, no longer suitable, several other models have been introduced. Organic, fluctuating models; human trajectories that are chaotic, libertarian, marginal. To die of hunger in this day and age, in a postmodern city like Montreal, you need to be disabled, dying, or stupid. Life doesn't give up easily. Although places where one can sleep in peace are increasingly rare, as soon as food is no longer a problem, nothing slows down the procession of the living.

Living beings congregate, assemble, spread disease, invent regimes, complain, vote, become indifferent, and disseminate ideas through media. A living being is a human billboard. A citizen, no matter how marginalized, is always the target of a pollster, the eventual consumer of fast food, the elemental part of a demographic to be conquered, a subculture to be infiltrated.

So I was a kind of well-integrated social wreck, a catastrophic scenario that would have been averted at the last minute, a mesclun of influences and abilities. This category of citizens is called "self-employed." A paradoxical term. Our self-reliance, or versatility if you like, is no doubt an indication of our vulnerability in the face of life's difficulties.

I didn't have any choice. I was always looking for work. The general idea was to get somewhere. Not to finish a race or follow a path to the end, but to go with the flow, do what was necessary to keep following the parade, struggling in the current. Paying for the electricity that would light up the occasional conversation.

Okay then, four manuscripts to condemn today.

How should I do it? Be succinct or use a more formal approach? Let's go with the usual tactic, which proves that I've done my job.

Three paragraphs, two paragraphs, a few lines and a page to

give my impressions, convey my dashed expectations (I don't actually have any expectations, but engaging in this literary sport keeps writers on their toes), communicate my criticism or distaste. Because reading can be distasteful, like overripe fruit, a badly seasoned dish, a failed recipe.

The author promises a fine soufflé, but right from the start, we bite into a dry biscuit. Spelling mistakes feel like mouldy wedges; obese sentences ooze; clichés resemble Smarties sold in bags in the candy aisle; bad dialogues are puff pasty swimming in a halo of animal fat; bad chapter titles look like dried-up maraschino cherries. A mediocre manuscript is a soulless pastry left behind in a flimsy stall. Makes me think of the Portuguese pastries sold on the Main, arranged in rows on wooden boards, heaps of flour assembled into indistinguishable bells, shouting their soulless flaky misery to onlookers.

For a few seconds, a bad manuscript can make you angry. Rage blows out of your nostrils. Once these few seconds pass, only a sense of sadness remains, a feeling of pity. As soon as the manuscript is put away in my large bag and my reports are printed, I sit down.

From all my time as a professional reader, I don't remember one categorical rejection that found another taker, that was published by another publisher or discovered under the gravel of its pitiful presentation. I am fully aware that I'm flushing the (unrealistic) hopes of four people down the drain, that I'm getting ready to disappoint four citizens who wish to distinguish and make a name for themselves, to become something other than anonymous figures knocking on people's doors with a census or plastic objects or handmade wallets for sale.

Typically, neither the managing editor nor the publisher

deign to get their hands dirty in the greasy pile of unsolicited manuscripts. A second chance is given to people they know, which makes the entire decision-making structure somewhat unfair. But, ultimately, publishers don't want to lose their reputation and will more often than not reject manuscripts written by their friends or acquaintances that received a poor assessment from the editorial board. In any event, in the worst cases, a bootlicking author that is rejected yet encouraged by a publisher's nepotism must submit to the multiple rewrites that a badly begun book necessitates. My work then serves no purpose, and I always feel a bit stunned when this type of book appears in stores. That said, the reviews and disappointing sales of the volume soon corroborate my initial assessment. Most of the time, I'm bang on.

I say it again and will keep saying it until the day I die: we have to read and keep reading, asking questions, gathering materials, getting informed. We often forget that a writer is an artist—of language, of documentation—an artist-reader.

Everyone is capable of reminiscing about life, summarizing a film, or retelling a story heard the night before. But the artist-reader transforms these ordinary narrative functions into unusual tableaus, long candlelit vigils, or solar, tousled, intriguing poems with repetitions that carry much weight like rails.

A thousand definitions of the writer exist.

Here, of course, I give myself permission to establish my point of view as a universal principle. That's all. I wouldn't go any further.

The issue is complex, but the method of investigation is

ultra simple. Ultimately, it's a matter of sounding out the water's surface, probing the abyss with sonar, grasping what lies beneath falsity and mannerisms. I love the idea of prospecting. It's useful. Because it involves the ideas of the sieve, gravel, and gold.

I often reassure my friends, who are sometimes outraged by my categorical rejections, with this maxim I invented: *No manuscript is lost, only memories with no author are.*

* * *

It's turning into comfortable indecency.

I was still into Maldonne. Mixed friendships, especially if they have a sexual or at least libidinal basis (isn't this always the case?), transform into bitter concoctions.

We never refuse someone something with impunity.

The imagination is limited to formulating trivial excuses. Once the rhetorical mechanism of forgiveness is set in motion, the matter seems settled. But this attitude is puerile. Besides, who among us (please raise your hand and say "I swear" three times without batting an eye) would be able to come up, time and again, with the right amount of words that a cordial understanding between two individuals requires? Few among us would. Very few. We all mess up. Our bodies betray us, arrogance gets the better of us, we fade into the carpet or in time. Life entails a reactive continuum in which we must swim of our own accord and knowledge. Who hasn't almost drowned? Who hasn't done an about turn that spatters everyone else?

Maldonne reacted with torturous frankness: she was way too late.

Time is celestial punishment. It acts as chastisement. Whoever imposes their routine on us is in fact asking us to adopt their lifestyle. Quite simply, the person imposes their rhythm on us. We have to adjust, to politely endure the discrepancy and renounce our use of time. Henceforth, the person stipulates belatedly, I will manage the time between us. Because controlling time comes under the jurisdiction of an almost political mania, a materialist mania that consists in passing judgment on how days and hours elapse. Which is odd, first of all, and if we think about it more carefully, rather rude. Because time is not a material but a universal pool of emptiness into which we pour everything that passes through our hands: death, illness, money, intelligence, trustworthiness, laziness, virtuosity, calm, relaxation, ease, stress, exercise, rejection, complicity, agony, and gratitude. If it's not a material but a flow of words we try to put in order so as to indicate who we are, then time is a subtle instrument of domination that we brandish when needed in order to establish our power and, consequently, our individualism. In prison, we do time because our power to dominate has been taken away from us, and this is how we recharge, by reconnecting to memories throughout the years. Memories = time; time = domination. More memories mean more domination; more time to devote to memories means more memories stored up.

Every lateness elicits an analysis. No lateness is trivial. In the case that concerns us, Maldonne used the opportunity to scold me. Every temporal punishment, from life imprisonment to a short delay, is the sign of a wrongdoing that must be atoned for, paid for. Making someone wait unexpectedly is always a punishment. We inflict dead time. The offence is concomitant with how long the person is made to wait.

2. THE GOSPEL OF DISTRIBUTION

As for me, her late arrival (in this case, to the screening of *Lemming* by Dominik Moll) added an additional annoyance: she would make me miss the beginning of the film. Fortunately, our friendship was protected by a few rules of goodwill, which we did not hesitate to use, such as the one stipulating that any lateness to a film or show authorized the person on time to depart from their function of the "waiter" and grab a seat in the theatre with no hard feelings.

Given our situation as cultural workers with numerous deprivations, neither one of us had a cell phone. The tacit, amicable agreement, the patiently created precedent of our sensual friendship, provided for the resolution of these misdemeanours.

But the damage was done.

For some unknown, metaphysical reason, I found that our difficult yet sensual relationship deserved to be protected, manicured, waxed. I stubbornly continued to blow hot and cold, without ever disconnecting our relations from the central heating block. We regularly imposed mutual torture on one another, each taking turns under the covers, admitting our mistakes yet continually repeating them, like comic book characters. No doubt, we liked fooling around. I couldn't grasp all the motives. One thing is certain: I thought of a sports analogy whenever those to whom I recounted our story inevitably asked the same questions. In my opinion, we were playing an interminable tennis match in which no winner ever seemed to emerge. A surrealist tennis match, reduced to a perpetual tie: advantage Ghislain, tie, advantage Maldonne, tie. Our mutual inability to know how to win a set transformed us into paradoxical adversaries. Who knew when the other would falter? we each wondered.

* * *

Ghislain is a loner. A hermit who is afraid of women. I don't say this out of bravado, or to brag. I just know it.

I had sex with him. No guy ever refuses the advances of a bold woman. That's all. It's enough! It's not like I'm looking for some good cock or a teddy bear. I have needs and I express them.

For me, Ghislain is a question mark on two feet.

I haven't become *persona non grata* because I missed our last movie date, have I?

Am I too demanding or too naughty? Does he see me as a castrating bitch? Ugh, horrible, he sees me as a castrating bitch. I've given him castration anxiety. No! Me, a castrating bitch! I hope this isn't how he sees me.

And anyway, this film *Lemming*, with the small rodent caught in the S-bend of the kitchen sink, is totally anal, totally castrating (Charlotte Gainsbourg's character, who suffers from a split personality and sleeps with her husband's boss, but also everything else that happens in the film, is enveloped in dreams, nightmares, dual personalities). The film itself suffers from castration anxiety. It prevaricates while seeking the viewer's orifice. Embarrassed with its hard-on, its semi-hard-on.

Must I take off, isolate myself on the islands of Denmark, follow the characters' journey in Aquin's *Hamlet's Twin*, suffer from all the existential angst and transform into an Ophelia of ice?

Is it my turn to compose my own *Antiphonary*, my book of solemn, liturgical chants to better avoid good old psychoanalytical atheism?

All this is disorienting.

Why does this old knowledge bother me all of a sudden, why does it cast a spell on me? I'm getting off track. It's coming back now. I was starting to get off track. I *am* getting off track. Okay! Okay, look, he'll get his chance. I'll give him a chance. It's not possible. I know that things are reciprocal. It's not as though I sensed his nervousness under the table or felt his knees shake as a symptom of his stupid fears. Being afraid of women is totally stupid. He's not afraid. He's not stupid. He just has some kind of mental block, some grief. That's all.

He is sullen, passive, pensive, but not stupid. Okay, then. I'll be patient. It'll be my turn. I made him angry. That's for sure. Maybe he thinks I don't respect him?

I'll wait for him to call me. I won't play the penitent woman.

But first, to not let things fester in misunderstanding and hang in the air, I need to set things straight.

A ten-word email will do.

*   *   *

This morning, I woke up with Robert De Niro's mindset in *The Mission*. I'm seeking one more reader.

My fists are tense.

I stiffen into a farmyard prophet, a rooster, having felt the ridiculousness of missionary zeal seize me. Anyone with a mission gets worked up, becomes awkward.

Since I woke up, this project has seemed undeniably relevant. I needed a counterpart, a counterweight, a second side to my life as a prospector-reader condemned, for the most part, to read bad manuscripts. Acid/base, black/white, yin/yang, you name it; on the one hand, I would look for manuscripts, and on the other, I would try to recruit readers.

* * *

That was all. It was simple, almost trivial. I needed to recruit readers for the authors I had liked.

We place too much emphasis on publication.

But this is only the start of the problem. As soon as the book is put into circulation, the hunt for readers begins. The hunting expedition is expected to end only when every potential reader has been exposed, if only for a few hours, to the book in question. An impossible challenge, undoubtedly riddled with problems. The life of a book is determined by the number of people who spontaneously transform it into a relay race.

Every book is conceived as a particular attractor, a unique character evolving on the heath of books. Labyrinthine, the world of books looks just like an underground city governed by writer-lords or book-lords, the newborns and translated immigrants enriching the social fabric, which is always in motion, never circumscribed.

I realized I was a scout. I felt like an agitated squirrel.

I could have asked Alberto Manguel to come to my rescue, could have summoned him to spread the good word about Quebecois books, about the richness of our French culture set in its beautiful American case. But this wasn't his cup of tea. Literary decorum demanded readers first be offered the canon, the vulgate, the Deuteronomy. Three or four authors, never more, form the base of a national literature. This great triumvirate or quatriumvirate usually represents the amount of literary knowledge required to claim that we know the literature of a country, province, or region in the world.

And even two suffice! Spain? Cervantes and García Lorca. The United States? Melville and Whitman.

And yet it's reductive to think we know Montreal after only seeing Old Montreal, the Olympic Stadium, and Sainte Catherine Street. What about Verdun? The Pointe-aux-Prairies Nature Park, Promenade Bellerive, Bois-d'Anjou, Parc île Haynes, or the beautiful shores of Senneville or Baie-d'Urfé? In this regard, knowing a city means continuing to traverse it, to walk it without blinders on and without prejudice, avoiding the media and tourist trenches.

But I was talking about books.

At best, I was going to unearth forgotten works, give them a second life; at worst, I was going to distribute works that have lost the right to survive in commercial bookstores.

In principle, I would first need to convert someone who despised fiction: Pascal.

* * *

To: readmeagain@sympatico.ca
From: earnestoearnesto@gmail.com

Dear Ghighi,

The show didn't keep me in the end. I don't care. I had fun. That's the main thing.

I read *Alia* by Mélikah Abdelmoumen last night. Pure guilty pleasure. Short, light-hearted novel with amusing literary love. Some novelists nowadays can be read quickly, like a good dose of sugar candy for the spirit. One of the literary characters, a film subtitler, totally delighted me. Imagine the witticism of such a character. I would've liked it even more if this novelist-neurotic character who was tormented by her parents suddenly lost her mind and got transformed into Dr. Jekyll and Mr. Hyde (Manguel's *A Reading Diary*... you told me to read it you shrewd devil... you're looking for mentors (*The Adventures of Telemachus* by Fénelon, a didactic treatise written in the guise of a novel, in which we discover the character of Mentor, the benevolent tutor whose name has come to mean "an experienced and trusted adviser or guide"). Do you remember when Manguel mentions that the *I* (our French *je*) stands between the *H* of Hyde and the *J* of Jekyll! An amusing semantic discovery, don't you think? The *I* disguised between the *H* and *J*... I would add between the *H* of *Hatred* and the *J* of *Jealousy*. We could go on. I love word teasers...)

Yes, this character should have invented subtitles, rewritten her own film. A novelist, it's possible... anyway, yes... she could have ventured into the unknown and let her Sapphic imagination flow... Let's say her feminine imagination first and secondly Greek and thirdly poetic and fourthly passionate about a sensuality that is perverse or pleasing, depending on the country where you use the word. Well, anyway, you'll see...

Why have I turned into a reviewer of Quebecois literature? Because you told me your secret. Well, actually, Pascal told me your secret. You want to become a proselytizer. You want to spread the good word of Quebecois literature... So I feel justified in giving you my reading observations. Pascal found your convictions pretty entertaining... You remind me of the president of UNEQ... always standing at attention, manly, sensitive, and with a hint of jazz-revolutionary desperation in the eyes, a man who draws his pen faster than his shadow moves, Stanley Péan is the Lucky Luke of book distribution in Quebec... But ever since that inscrutable François Avard proclaimed in *ICI* that Quebecois literature is dull and that the *Devoir's* book section looked like *The Catholic Register*, we can understand why people like Péan are necessary. They reset the clock, build the clock, play clockmakers, and repair the clock... You know as well as I do that the clock of Quebecois literature looks more like Poe's pendulum... made to torture all those who approach it with impunity... Sugar-coated torture, fidgeting on Radio-Canada... Basket of verse...

Pascal finds you really funny... He told me that you recommended he read *Le Grand Khan* by Jean Basile... You, you little agitator, tried to tell him that the novel was in no way a history book about the emperor of the Mongols... Not historical at all, rather a slice of life of several characters, written in a flowing, telegraphic language, a page-turner with no bathroom breaks... Your effort delighted him so much that he's given in.

I'll read it too and we'll get together?

Wasn't Basile a Russian homosexual? And a former journalist for *La Presse*? Didn't he die of AIDS?

By the way, Pascal thought it would be a good idea to have a *Grand Khan* get-together at his place next Saturday. You're not working at the Liposuction Slushie on Saturday, are you?! Saturday at Pascal's, we'll erect an altar to the literature from *here*, we'll fashion our precious ones, Huysmans-style, we'll build a dazzling turtle of a thousand sapphires whose remote-controlled mission will be to bite the legs of people who mope...

Ciao!

Courrège
xx

.

3.

LAVERDURE THE PARROT

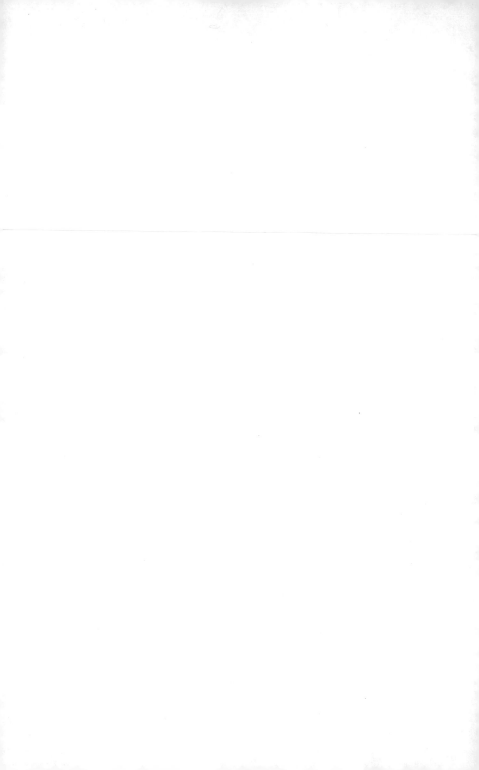

PASCAL'S SMALL APARTMENT.
The calm clamour of the street.
No troubles. No blockheads. Music: Chick Corea, "Steps –
What Was" from *Now He Sings, Now He Sobs*, 1968, Blue Note.
The door opens and closes three times. Maldonne looks at
the fridge, patters around the kitchen, heads for the bathroom. First bar. Courrège, shy, in a freeze frame, hangs back
near the entrance and the living room. Pascal, courteous,
shows her his collection of Baroque CDs. A piano clangs
and pounds in the background. Increasing speed. Suspended
notes. Ghislain's mind is spinning. He's ready. Not sure for
what. But he's ready. The music moves his feet implicitly,
secretly sneaks into his metacarpi.

They launch into the slow chaos of get-togethers and conversations. They dive in. Confident. Pascal makes a witty remark. Courrège brightens up. The signal is given, the group forms. Maldonne returns to the living room. Ghislain doesn't speak to her yet. They wait for words, they wait for topics, viewpoints, the upward curve of laughter and alcohol.

Beer is secured from the fridge at a steady pace. Maldonne hurries to get it, uncomfortable. Offers one to Ghislain out of reflex. Ghislain grabs the bottle and turns his back on her. Thirty-year-old adolescents; it's touching.

They sketch out patterns, lose their discomfort in fits and starts, peripherally at first, then moving into the centre. The music gives an order to battle, suggests certain measures. They won't go there yet. There's a theme. It's true. They have gathered for a reason. The torrent of tension gives way to an attempt at cohesion. It's time. Ghislain pulls up a chair. Briefly tries to draw the others' attention. In vain. Forward move. Courrège is listening. But she's the only one. She reflects during a short drum solo. Pascal delivers replies, chooses an interlocutor; the conversation settles into good-natured sarcasm. They still don't know much yet. They hesitate. Chick Corea releases tremulous sound waves, Felliniesque colours into the nest. Everyone is talking. To the walls. While laughing. Pascal speaks. He has the floor. He charms because he speaks his mind and targets his interlocutors. And sometimes he doesn't speak his mind. He knows. He's got it. He arouses relief, a laugh, ease. He knows. Controlling the humour of the situation, he's not a materialist for nothing. Has all he needs to become a courtier. He knows it, has read Baldassare Castiglione.

The pendulum swings, leaves the music behind. A wild note gives them hope of some kind of emulsion. They are deluding themselves, but they're having fun. Ghislain crumbles. Keyed up. Courrège, who gets along equally well with Pascal and Ghislain, throws in a question that's high up on the evening's agenda. More beer, please. Skip the decorum. Pascal echoes the *la*, drums the beat with his fingers, mimics Corea with his voice. Everything winds around and remains for a moment under their feet, in their hands. Courrège shifts gears, drinks slowly, states the four steps of devotion: patience, grace, verbal ability, and adult candour. While sacred, hirsute vessels may reign on a distant dresser in Pascal's bedroom, they're not yet shaping the sorcery of the evening.

COURRÈGE: This is a reading party...

GHISLAIN: Did everyone find the book?

MALDONNE: No problem.

PASCAL: Good old library and archives cataloguing.

GHISLAIN: No one bought it?

MALDONNE: What for?

GHISLAIN: I'd rather buy books. I don't like pecking about in library copies.

COURRÈGE: What's important is reading the thing, not owning it.

GHISLAIN: No, borrowing bothers me.

PASCAL: Strange way of thinking.

GHISLAIN: I'm not a fetishist.

MALDONNE: I think you are a bit. It's important to see things as they are.

GHISLAIN: Things are fine as they are.

PASCAL: Anyway, I read *Le Grand Khan*.

MALDONNE: What did you think?

PASCAL: Basile's not a bad writer. I loved the portrait of Montreal in the '60s, the old Kresge stores, Dorchester Street—his book is a user's manual of walking. It's also dense. He doesn't want to give us time to breathe; he thrashes about like a demon in a web of cultural references. I liked it.

GHISLAIN: But it's fiction. You just read some fiction and liked it?

PASCAL: I'm not narrow-minded, Ghis. I read historical tomes and biographies, but that's not why I refuse to see films by Todd Haynes, Emmanuel Mouret, or Paul Thomas Anderson. You literary people are funny. You live according to fixed principles. Fiction is organic, isn't it? Just like life?

GHISLAIN: I thought you hated novels and poetry.

PASCAL: Hold on, I didn't say I read poetry. I don't know anything about poetry. That's a fact. But still, just because I don't know anything about a genre doesn't mean I can't appreciate it. It's just a question of exposure.

Courrège removes the Corea CD and looks through the stacked cases of copied music, takes out John Zorn's *Protocols of Zion.*

Soon they'll start playing variations of the current exchanges, but they know, everyone knows, that the parrot lies in wait. They hear a tapping on the window. The clang of a ring against a glass pane. Almost imperceptible. Zorn delivers his score of exercises in cinematographic style. Zorn in the apartment and a tapping on the window that no one hears.

They rant and rave, then someone needs to go to the dep: they're out of beer. Ghislain asks them which chips to get. Whatever, as long as they're salty. The parrot is still tapping on the window. No one hears it. The conversation has gotten back on track; Basile's book reaches out, opens eyes, brings up citations, begins to unite the mobile readers by subsuming them.

Maldonne heads to the kitchen. Discreet, hand on the door handle. Then, when she opens the door, her eyes meet the parrot. She jumps.

MALDONNE: Hey! Come see! What's going on? There's a parrot in the kitchen!

GHISLAIN: What!

No one knows what to do: open the window; call the SPCA, the fire department, a taxi; take off running; or admit their fondness for bird hunting.

PASCAL: Ghislain, go get my leather gloves from the hallway closet. The large, black leather gloves. We should at least try to bring it inside.

MALDONNE: You're sure it's safe?

COURRÈGE: Parrots have really sharp beaks!

GHISLAIN (returning with the gloves): What you're doing is illegal... If an accident happened, how would you... It must be someone's, there's no parrot nest up on Mont Royal, it's got to be someone's... Maybe it has a ring around its claw. Is there a ring around its claw?

PASCAL: No, there's nothing that looks like a tag or a marker... Okay, protect your eyes! I'm opening the window!

The parrot swoops into the kitchen, madly flapping its wings. Pascal panics, trying not to show it, but his arms keep the beat of a paradoxical polka. Maldonne takes cover under the white kitchen table, Courrège clears off to the living room, Ghislain plays his role of saviour of Quebec literature by closing the bathroom door from the kitchen hubbub, which has momentarily transformed into a *Benny Hill* scene.

The parrot croaks ad infinitum:
Chatter, chatter, that's all you ever do! Chatter, chatter, that's all you ever do! Chatter, chatter, that's all you ever do! Chatter, chatter, that's all you ever do! Chatter, chatter, that's all you ever do! Chatter, chatter, that's all you ever do! Chatter, chatter, that's all you ever do! Chatter, chatter, that's all you ever do!
Flap-flap, the clamour of fowl.
Chatter, chatter, that's all you ever do! Chatter, chatter, that's all you ever do!...
And it goes on like this for an hour.

* * *

Life without danger is life without art.

Case in point: A parrot on the guest list. And not just any parrot. Laverdure the parrot, straight out of *Zazie in the Metro*, Queneau's cult classic. A drivelling chatterbox, like any good, old parrot, invading our active mental space, eliminating in the blink of an eye all the work I had done to make this *Grand Khan* evening happen. A bad sign.

Pascal cut in: "We have to call the SPCA."

On the face of it, it all seemed compromising and ill-advised. I was jealous of the virile self-confidence of this man who had undoubtedly caught Maldonne at the turnstile and caught up with Courrège in the tunnel. I started imagining all kinds of scenarios à la Belmondo, the amused legionary's roguish expression and remarks. A bad mix.

Maldonne cooed, silently aloof. Everything was taking on the magnitude of a comic drama, though directed by Wong Kar-Wai. An aesthetic drama with characters who strike a pose and a languorous narrator who strikes it too. A melancholic drama with a surreal aura.

Laverdure the parrot wreaked havoc; it was the price to pay for fiction.

Raising my voice, I managed to make myself heard: "Listen to me for a moment... Courrège, you read *Zazie in the Metro*, didn't you? Remember Laverdure the parrot? Remember that tiresome parrot? Come on... you must remember... Maldonne? Do you know...?"

I went on: "Courrège, you saw that film by Louis Malle, didn't you? Where Philippe Noiret plays the role of the transvestite Gabriel. Come on, remember the jump cuts, the burlesque scenes, and the awkward face of Zazie, dressed in red? Come on... the parrot in the apartment... the parrot at the bar... shit."

Finally, Courrège reacted. She remembered Louis Malle's film and Philippe Noiret but had forgotten the parrot's existence. Maldonne hadn't seen the film, and Pascal, who knew his film history and had read about Malle, pretended not to know anything until I pressed him...

Like a lord calling for a lull, Pascal described the scene with the parrot drinking grenadine. We talked briefly about the film's high-quality editing, whose action takes place during a subway strike in Paris. Marceline's ethereal presence, her still face, steady feet, her body being moved on a dolly, the static camera. Excellent directing.

The diversion over, we turned to the matter at hand.

PASCAL: Some literary person or cinephile took it upon himself to teach his parrot the phrase. Not paying attention, he must have opened his window and the bird escaped. That's all.

GHISLAIN: But what if I'm right and this is the character from the book come to interfere in our lives? And why not? We were meeting to discuss a forgotten book that still deserves our attention, *Le Grand Khan*, and here comes a parrot, strangely similar to Queneau's parrot, knocking on our door. We have awoken ghosts.

PASCAL (*addressing the others with an amused gleam and a "don't-blame-me-I'm-sympathetic-at-heart" look*): Okay, okay. Fine! Who was right and who was wrong, and why, and what would it mean, anyway? The situation was ridiculous, and the ridiculous can be explained in only two ways: a celestial and divinatory way and a sherlockholmesque and deductive way. No other choice.

GHISLAIN (*surprised at himself*): I want to take care of the parrot! He's mine! I'll take him to my place! Make way, please! I'll take all the responsibility.

Pascal, used to the quantum leaps of my thinking, didn't raise an eyebrow. He told me to stay calm until we call the SPCA. It was the thing to do with this lost parrot. A parrot is a very expensive bird. Very very very very very very expensive. There was nothing to wonder about; we were dealing with some rich man or an eccentric with deep pockets.

Pascal's perspective warranted us to call it a night. I stopped too, like everyone else, definitely humiliated, my *Grand Khan* in tow, ego slightly bruised. We decided as a group that the parrot would stay in the kitchen. We had decided to take care of it, in high style, in accordance with the laws of creaturely hospitality.

But I had my plan. I slipped away quietly.

3. LAVERDURE THE PARROT

* * *

Night had fallen over Montreal and I couldn't sleep.

The soldiers defending Quebecois literature, I knew them all. In my cosy bed, curled up under the sheets, I saw them—gangs of mercenaries, Kalashnikovs slung over their shoulders, eyes sharp and cruel, glowing with their momentous mission.

At the depot of annual sales reports, the poor, disillusioned and humiliated authors who had not managed to sell off at least 300 copies of their tomes (a quantity that transforms shame or humiliation into moderate success) would be given the right to enlist potential readers.

The forms would clearly stipulate that to approach readers who were particularly recalcitrant or insensitive to the type of book offered would be a violation subject to fines. In other words, the form would include an entire paragraph that defined the word "potential," intended to dampen the passion of fanatical writers and their recruitment campaigns. Not so crazy. It would be the paradox and the law. Since paradox and law often sleep in the same bed, this shouldn't surprise you.

The poor writer-hunter, rifle in hand, would go in search of *potential* readers in parks, supermarkets, deps, libraries, universities, colleges, and shoe stores. And presto, you would be recruited.

I'm in Montreal in 2006 and formulating empty words.

You don't need to have the most enlightened perspective. You just need to read, watch TV, go geocaching, share a room with the "Fucking Maniac with an Axe" in the *Horror Movies' Shocking Chatroom*. Nothing is fragile. Everything transforms.

Where am I in all of this?

And this damn parrot, Laverdure? My plan.

My plan was full of holes but breathtakingly simple. My sides on fire, my feet on fire, my insides (I don't know anymore). I was intoxicated. The only thing I saw on my twenty-one-inch mental screen was Laverdure the parrot.

My plan had been inspired by reading *Extractor 568*, a small little book published by Jean Skelton Books, as part of their Cherokee Series.

Small, strange, post-exotic books. See, for example, *Zulu*—the first one with Michael Caine, of course, not the others. A certain Mime Wotan had written this short novel (his first book, in fact).

Today, people talk about the short novel, a genre which has also been called short prose, novella, or novelette. Anyway, it was a short novel of about thirty pages. But it would be stupid of me to talk about it. It's better that you read it for yourselves, without preamble.

Imagine: A world of angry, disappointed, proliferating writers, beating a path to posterity, who, over the years and due to overcrowding (a myth, it seems, but also an inexhaustible source of narrative paranoia), would have earned the right to temporarily kill their critics.

All this in the hopes of controlling the interest in autochthonous literature, let's say in a (post–Jacques Godbout) future era, a literature that's rather forsaken and sadistically relegated to the Ministry of the Survival of Regional Cultures. Thus, among these supraquebecois autochthonous authors (with several generations of interracial mixing invalidating any description of this new type of ordinary citizen), the most deserving would be granted the right to eliminate a certain number of their literary enemies, while keeping within reasonable and pre-established quotas. Wotan had written what science fiction experts call a dystopia (the opposite of a utopia, where all is well).

* * *

Mime Wotan

Extractor 568

—

CHEROKEE SERIES

Jean Skelton Books

Jean Skelton Books
6366 St-Hubert Street
Montreal, QC H2S 2M2
www.jeanskeltonbooks.com

Legal deposit second quarter 2006
Bibliothèque et Archives nationales du Québec

LIBRARY AND ARCHIVES
CANADA CATALOGUING IN PUBLICATION

Wotan, Mime, author
Extractor 568 / Mime Wotan

ISBN 978-29807-842-73

CHAPTER I

—

Ezekiel Bradeau,
scribwrit

My name is Ezekiel Bradeau and I kill readers who don't like my books.

Twenty a month, that's my quota.

I use the Extractor 568. An old model. It identifies contempt within an eight-kilometre radius. No one wants to work with these slightly dated machines anymore. It doesn't bother me.

All my novels deserve consideration.

I live in a greedy, rotten world, inclined to excess. A large strip of land called the Quebec Isle.

The market and school circuit. Many neighbourhoods in sight. Sometimes I walk for hours before attempting a capture.

I kill by pseudo-direct osmosis, old-school style.

I set the Extractor 568 to the red indicator light. Geometric shapes appear. The key to it all rests in the moment just before the signal. When the indicator light flashes and detects the presence of a tenacious, contemptuous thought on my screen (the thought has to be tenacious, since my model is not powerful enough to detect fleeting thoughts), I have my victim.

There are many of us.

Proliferating negative thoughts. I don't speak Chineaise or Spanishola.

No need to stare at the moon, still too close, to determine my absent-mindedness. I sort, I walk, I write some more.

Now all publishing workstations are free. Since I can, I go. There are chairs by the green machines. First I think up the text, then I write, as quickly as possible, before the sentinels shoot arrows at me.

An arrow again. It barely grazes me. I dictate the story of my sentinel to an invisible being. A good topic, these sentinels. No nose, huge eye sockets, long forked tongue. They speak Chineaise and Spanishola. I speak Eng-Fren.

They call me archaic. I use junk words, concept words. I find them in philosophie books.

En tout cas. Bombyx is gone. The Chief of the Quebec Isle Territories. Beautiful reservation. All the rights. We can kill those who feel contempt for us, give Eng-Fren language classes to the lost ones; it pays. Papa Dragonfly from Chicoutimi just gave a talk written on zebra parchment. Stretch out the zebra parchment, and presto, a lecture. We hear many lectures on the res. Many scribwrits. Papers multiply, we don't belong to ourselves anymore; we now read our thoughts in public. You have to kill to live better, have more space.

Let's get back to my story about the sentinel. I imagine him as a boa constrictor trying to steal my ideas. We have no more boas than cows here. Only insects and some deer. Lemur pastry, ant pâté, cockroach cookies, rat brochettes, earthworm flour. With every crunchy biscuit, I collect myself. Go quiet, stifle noise.

The sentinel shoots another arrow at me. Not interested in my sentinel story; a bad book; a really bad book.

I take out my Extractor 568.

The sentinel suddenly becomes ant food.

He falls on the ground.

I focus on my books, whatever you might say about them.

Who speaks Eng-Fren nowadays? Best to keep your extractor on at all times, contempt proliferates everywhere.

A sentinel that transforms into a boa then strokes its master. It works. Simplicity is the best idea. A denouement is brief. A boa kills, and if it doesn't kill, it becomes a book.

I write one book a day. I am a regular scribwrit. My book, in several hands.

And I kill, I have my card. I shape lives by scraping off the excess fungus.

Ever since the hunt for contempt began, religion ended.

I didn't get lucky when they handed out the machines. Got an old model. The new models also eliminate critics who write negative reviews.

The sentinel calls out to me again. He has regained consciousness. Now he is brand new. He speaks to me in Chineaise. I don't understand anything. I pretend to be plugging in my air purifier.

Stated in bastardized Chineaise:

The book is just paper.

Killing doesn't mean anything anymore, ever since we started giving them new life. I kill, I reset. I kill, they are reborn.

To obtain a Permit 4, you need to become an artisan who is essential to the community. Then killing becomes a real hunt.

One day, I will get my Permit 4.

Fabien Makakrista lives his life as a man of letters by killing those who hurt him. It's reassuring. I've always managed by plugging into a memory keeper. So said a philosophe between two bawdy tunes. Makakrista sees only fire. I am still alive. It's because his machines are stupid. I'm not referring to him, of course; I'm only saying that his machines are stupid. Not him. Makakrista is sweetness itself and raw talent. He loves books. He devours them, but he writes them even better. He kills because he's not wrong to do it. He is a genius. We get along well.

Makakrista has his Permit 4. I will have mine, too.

When the Institute for the Struggle Against Contempt was founded, I was not yet born. I hadn't even been conceived by my parents alpha and beta yet. Life has been good ever since. We don't say "That sucks," "I don't like it," "He's an ass," "What a phoney!" We abstain and we write.

The lousier it is, the more we must write it. When we read, it is to escape.

But we have to keep killing the contemptuous, because they increase the ambient levels of animosity a great deal. I am a scribwrit who has understood his utility.

Today I can walk with impunity in all the neighbourhoods of the tribe without being overly subjected to the sentinels' arrows, to the internal invectives of disappointed readers, precisely because I've been carrying the Extractor 568 in my bag for a while now. At the beginning, I didn't always have it on me. I was afraid the device would malfunction. What if it actually killed? I dreamed of having a Permit 4. I was confident in my ability as a scribwrit; I had passed all of the Institute's tests without any difficulty. A typical case, decent human warmth, definite talent, normal capacity for judgment. I was ready to watch the screen, assess the flashing light. A consolation, on the one hand; pruning shears, on the other. Every morning, I watched the sun appear on my balcony. It was beautiful, serene, the humiliations forgotten.

I played the game of an accomplished scribwrit. We enjoy life with Permit 3. We write in the morning or the evening, reread what we've written, then *bzzz*, publish it immediately. An enormous paper-pusher right on my street corner. It could have been noisy with the machine around, but instead, exhilarating melodies, enchanting frictions poured out of this immense box of new metal. I like the sound of printers getting down to work.

That which pushes the paper into the trays, binds, glues, stamps, expedites in all directions.

Great finds.

Contempt was the key, the engine driving all my searches. An extensively developed science.

CHAPTER II

The Founding of the Institute for the Struggle Against Contempt

Over many years. Since the year in multiples of ten and of sixty, as well. All systems of societal survival have been summed up in one: the struggle against contempt.

Think of the nursery rhymes learned in grade school: "No contempt, no contempt, it's no good for making friends."

I only know what it is like to live in barbarian times. But human beings don't change. Not yet. They multiply, yes, but they don't change. The worst response is to increase the worst tenfold. Today, everything rests on the shoulders of scribwrits. The era that synthesized light and paper has transformed the idea our ancestors had of distribution. Paper is practical. It's not cumbersome, it's thin, it rips and burns and holds ideas. An excellent invention! The best technology since the beginning of time.

The survival of communities, especially the smallest ones

like ours, depended on the implementation of an anti-contempt campaign.

What exactly is contempt? What does it consist of? Why this obsession with contemptuous action? The philosophes have pondered it. Here's an excerpt from Notebook 8 on the contemptuous instinct:

"Contempt was born in an ancient epoch of the animal kingdom, at a time when violence and physical aggression were not enough to control all aspects of communal life. Contempt is an adjuvant, a lack, an inability transformed into a death wish. Finding it on our path means finding the origin of heart palpitations, unsatisfied vengeance, unmistakable hate and envy, domination. The pit of contempt stands at the core of incomprehension and ignorance. Extracting the essence of this principle, breaking down its foundations, is more than simply a duty for all. It is indispensable to social harmony. We must, however, remain vigilant. Contempt is protean. It changes as easily as a river's course.

This is why contempt, in all its forms, must be considered a constant menace, a call to slaughter—either pseudo-direct (by osmosis, Permit 3) or direct (Permit 4).

The survival of a specific community's culture, the harmony of a particular group, the wellbeing of the inhabitants of a pre-established territory, and the preservation of the principles of general knowledge of a given minority depend on extremely low levels of contempt circulating through its networks.

Teaching the principles of the struggle against contempt

will begin in grade school. Ignorance, arrogance, resentment, weakness, and unmotivated anger will be examined, analyzed, compiled.

Yet given that human beings are perfectible, passionate about contradiction, and generally, are prone to rebel against their own happiness, at times we will need to resort to artificial solutions and extreme measures. For this reason, we have determined different classes of citizens capable of handling anti-contempt devices.

Everyone has a right to a Type 1 permit. This means that any contemptuous attempt, manifestation of contempt, or contemptuous action could be noted in the file of the citizen in question if an aggrieved citizen deems it necessary. In short, everyone possesses a pocket-size Extractor 144 that catalogues all forms of contempt. At the end of the day, the extractor determines which ones need to be added to a citizen's file.

Permit 2 represents a transitional phase, through which one can eventually acquire Permit 3. A Permit 1 holder with an excellent anti-contempt file will be given the opportunity, after a few years, to apply for Permit 2. This permit grants one thing and one thing only: the right to non-ignorance. As knowledge can be a potential source of conflict, it is preferable that this permit be distributed to the least contemptuous people. This has led to the creation of an Institute for the Struggle Against Contempt.

The completion of a training program at the Institute for the Struggle Against Contempt eventually grants one the right to a Permit 3. Somewhat dangerous, but having almost no bearing on the mortality rate, this permit grants the right to instantaneously reprogram the occasional contemptuous character, using various extractors available (i.e., Models 500 to 967). For example, Model 834 allows users to vary the reprogramming pressure, while Extractor 967 allows them to search through barely formulated thoughts within a fifteen-kilometre radius. Partial brain death followed by an immediate rebirth are the typical phases experienced when one of these devices is used on others.

A minority of people are walking around with a Permit 3. Usually, it is the final permit granted by the Institute and constitutes a favour or privilege offered to those with exemplary files of non-ignorance.

But then what is a Permit 4? Who can obtain it and why?

The history of Permit 4 is somewhat nebulous. We know that it was approved by the members of the Institute only a short time ago, at most a few centuries. Permit 4 is the ultimate community resource. Each beneficiary may only use it about five times per year. It constitutes the last regulatory step of the ambient contempt level—the pure and simple extinction of the contemptuous unit. For use against this stage of hate, contempt, and repeat offence, a Permit 4 will be granted upon request to an exemplary Permit 3 holder (following a thorough, rigorous, long, and exhaustive examination of the user's accumulated contempt file and their non-ignorance points earned)."

The notebook never ends. Neither, it would seem, does Monsieur Dragonfly of Chicoutimi.

With his zebra parchment, he sermonizes. The entire Jolicoeur block listens—even the sentinels—to the book-free rhetoric emerging from his eradicated mouth. Old tongue with all and with too much.

One day, I will have blood on my hands after having to watch his charmante hairdo. Come to think of it, I'm starting to wander off topic like Dragonfly.

He declares on his zebra parchment: "I say unto you: the poet, seated for centuries, fought against the world's filth accumulated in her. The poet's sharp-edged thought cut absolute evil at the root. In the blood. In the eye. In the embryo. The poet ate herself from the inside. Devoured completely. Chewed and swallowed the bones and organs. With all the encrusted shit. The warrior poet cleared the air. And when she stands up from her chair, many centuries later, as I do now, do you think the Court will recognize her action?"

There are tears and there is spite. We hesitate. We think good is possible, then we branch off.

If I walk around the Jolicoeur block in the morning and I don't meet up with any contemptuous characters, the day feels long. No one stops doing contemptuous things just because they know that, even if they get caught, they will be resurrected for the better. It's the law of best action in a short period of time. It's the game of the chicken and the cleaver. But if I cut today, the body won't be the only one continuing to hop and run around out of instinct, but the head as well.

The immediacy of the rebirth sends shivers down the spine, but many like this feeling. Mothers compel their unruly children to be violently contemptuous against certain books written by Type 3 scribwrits. Everyone knows the Type 3s. They jeer at us all the time, it's practically a sport.

The sentinels are usually worn-out. Not more than the zebra parchments displayed here and there, but sometimes not less, either.

Their bodies regenerate often. They are habitually contemptuous. A tough, persistent contemptuous character, ready to give his time in the pursuit of others, will get his chance one day. He will be recruited.

My books don't look like anything in particular. Sometimes they have straight lines that invite danger. I don't pay any attention to the writing next door. Because there is always a scribwrit next door who scorns you a bit, makes you feel less certain of your talent. Then you wish you had a Permit 4. But you're happy enough with a 3. Most of the time, we kill each other by piecemeal contempt interspersed with rebirth. We become more precise, we stammer less, and our contempt loses its vehemence.

Only we try not to think too much about Makakrista. You shouldn't think too much about the Permit 4s. I don't dare write about them, in fact.

But I say things, I get carried away. The 4s don't really kill.

They await the bearers of diatribes more resilient than weeds.

The hands that soar while others withdraw, the swimmer's movements.

Scribwrits transform the raw energy of contempt, the harsh net of social orders and carriage returns, even in the glacial time of night, even though the sentinels have become an army of puppets harming all that moves in Jolicoeur, between the great streams of La Chine and the remnants of the Saint River. What happens there, despite death and contempt, the ruined books and the books that get read; what happens there, despite our Eng-Fren battles, despite my not understanding Chineaise and my desire for the Spanishola of the great showcases; what happens there moves all of life's turbines, all of Quebec Isle.

CHAPTER III

The Organic Library of the Isle

I, Ezekiel Bradeau, a little older, a lot more burdened, and dressed in a cacophony of abuse (the sound of my voice is conserved in a box, better this way, otherwise subject to exceedingly blatant contempt), I am a scribwrit. To begin with, I reap; it's like fishing, but the fish fly around me.

As soon as the noises leap, I hurry and type as quickly as possible to catch the flying phrases.

If I repeat myself too much, I'll have to curse Makakrista. It's simple when you understand life. So understand it.

All the land from La Chine Canal to Saint River is strewn with libraries.

Organic cement is more malleable than wood and slower to deteriorate.

The sentinels confront us, die in batches, and are reborn without too much trouble. The day after they're concocted, all the books written by Permit 3 scribwrits shoot off through the pneumatic tubes. A system that ends at the habitat doors.

The beauty of the thing is that every scribwrit has their preferred neighbourhood block. I never launch my catalogues of torture at random.

The map of contempt indicates areas of suffering and areas of indifference. Indifference is preferable. Everything we inject, the phrasal liquid, comes back to us through better veins.

Contempt obstructs; it doesn't want to let anything pass by.

Sometimes, the indifferent blocks begin to act contemptuously if a wave of contempt touches a habitat's corner.

The paradox is that contempt is adequately transmitted, even when indifference does not encourage the transmission.

In the scheme of things, 10% of one day's novelistic output returns to the organic libraries. No one consults these books anymore. Street vendors, prospectors, and peddlers deal with them. There are book stalls and book fairs. Prices fluctuate depending on the library fires. It's difficult to stop them. There are cycles and lulls, fire recessions and peak periods.

The remaining 90% returns to the pneumatic tubes the next day. People read, discard, buy, recycle, burn, raise prices, keep, burn again, make laws; there are always more scribwrits, then gradually the Permit 4s nab their Sunday trophies.

Every eliminated scribwrit has a right to a clay statue.

Every neighbourhood block has its patron saint.

On the roof of my habitat, I stowed away the statue of André Moreau. He is the patron of the sublime joy of being, as explained to scribwrits. A master thinker devotedly revered during our studies at the Institute, he had been one of us before we were what we became. His work is not as important as that of half the scribwrits today, but it was a precursor of the textual tone prescribed by the

Institute. He drove away the Chineaise and the Spanishols. He survived underground in the year 1000.

All of Quebec Isle is at his feet. We call him Sonny Berkeley or Smiling Faust.

He wrote: "I am so naive others think that my naïveté conceals something suspect, even dangerous. This is why they come from all over hoping to discover what new towering trick I am hiding in my bag, contrary to Marguerite de Navarre, who hid bags in her tricked-out tower."

I never fail to quote this exceptional being. At the Institute, we studied him as an expert weapon against contempt.

Contempt is a curious beast that dominates and crushes everything.

Acting contemptuously makes the contemptuous bigger. It is not a matter of staying small but of knowing one's size. Of frequently adjusting the rate of philosophie in the internal organs.

I've been shot by arrows. Sometimes the sentinels know how to aim, but this doesn't happen often; their devices are cumbersome and heavy.

The poor sentinel who hadn't yet spotted my Extractor 568 (sometimes, I admit, this device has its failings) launched an arrow in my direction. Stupid bastard. I tuned my extractor, and *brrrppp!* Down in the poppies! Resuscitated, and therefore returned to more positive sentiments, he offered me a fried rat biscuit. He had too many in his Chineaise lunchbox.

It was good to break bread with sentinels once in a while. I could dream, I had a right, I was a famous scribwrit. I had written three or four novels on controversial subjects— great sagas involving multiple rebuffed ties of affection between sentinels and scribwrits, between Permit 1s and Permit 4s. In my view, excellent anti-contempt work.

After the publication of these tomes, they called me a sensationalist, even a traitor. I had to empty the batteries of two Extractor 456s before managing to finish off all the contemptuous characters that spread the word! In return, I was reprogrammed so many times over this turbulent period that I lost the gift to hate. Now, I'm only parsimoniously contemptuous, showing a calculated refinement. At the source of all these battles, poor binary logic:

Contempt = obstacle; obstacle = destruction

Contempt hit home faster than a look, incited by controversy.

Of the actual output, as I have already explained, 10% end up in organic libraries. Yet a vast majority of books launched in the morning end up in different receptacles, scattered here and there at everyone's discretion, by evening.

Bottomless pits in which the book pulp coagulates—fading the ink, devouring the paper, digesting the fibres. At the end of the tubes, concealed beneath neon, cast iron covers, the abyss glows, the notorious bottom, the great lake of insignificance.

Reading Saint Louis-René des Forêts at the Institute in a course on death and the book, we learned this great truth: "In the final analysis, doesn't the omnitelling voice only reveal the vacuity of its inexhaustible flow? Perhaps its sole aim is to get lost in insignificance, the defeat duly recognized so as to stop receiving the validation of success, even if the same notion could designate that which, denied if not rejected for lacking consistency, should proscribe the usage."

"The vacuity of its inexhaustible flow," it was all there. The amazing prose of Saint LRdF in his *Pas à pas jusqu'au dernier.**

The sentinel is harassing me again, so I leave, taking my last seventy words with me.

Neon-lit Spanishol storefronts everywhere. Glass the colour of faded old gouache.

I walk around the vast Angrignon Park, home to the city's largest rat-breeding farm. Tons of these feisty and tasty

---

* *Step by Step Until the Last.* (Trans.)

vermin. Happy meat at the centre of life. Quick feet in the drums of their cages.

The meat paradox is the most curious one of all. To become meat, one has to be born, but to bear the name, one has to die.

As for me, I am tired of running. I arm my extractor, and the sentinel collapses.

* * *

Night, night, still night, still the sublime moment, still the face of Mary Magdalene superimposed on the dark TV screen. Love of literature, love of reading, I see it through a mystical face, a lost and found face, a Mary Magdalene, the age-old symbol of the repentant prostitute. The one who offers happiness indiscriminately, disregards ugliness, welcomes bodies between her expert hands the way souls were once received by the breath of the Holy Spirit.

Okay, I'm becoming a doddering old fool. I don't feel well. Or rather, I'm dissolving and reality is slipping way. At times, I'm overcome with disgust when I read. Saturated.

So I had a plan, yes, a plan. I was going to take care of Laverdure the parrot, re-educate it, bring it in line, transform it into an apostle of Quebec letters by training it.

Propelled by a sudden determination, I jump out of bed.

First, my face in the mirror. A splash of cold water, the towel, a swipe with the electric razor. Another splash of cold water. My life is restored. Eyes still slightly puffy, I examine myself. A free film, a film of immediate crystallization: the mirror is an astonishing ordeal. I stand there before it, letting my drowsiness go, rudely greeted by reality, already absorbed by others, by their view of my body, their interpretation of my condition, their opinion of my person. I stand there, Ghislain the reader, employed at the Couche-Tard dep at the Joliette subway stop, unknown to Antoine Doinel and Alice Pleasance Liddell.

No passing through the mirror before being completely awake.

I am Ghislain the reader, tired of rejecting manuscripts, newly convinced that Quebecois literature needs to be promoted by means other than the usual channels, an employee of the Couche-Tard dep at the Joliette subway stop and an unrepentant consumer of Yum Yum cheese sticks, preferably the 270 g bag. I avoid dietary recommendations and savour this discrepancy.

I refuse to read the ingredients of these famous cheese sticks. But then I read them anyway and here they are: these snack bites resemble strange bacteriological concretions with a somewhat fecal shape, simultaneously spongy, sticky, and solid, made from corn meal dipped in boiling canola oil, then seasoned with modified milk ingredients, maltodextrin, salt, and cheddar cheese powder (milk, bacterial culture, microbial enzymes, whey, maltodextrin, salt, buttermilk, citric acid, natural flavour, disodium phosphate, lactic acid), colour, monosodium glutamate, flavour (yeast extract), citric acid, lactic acid, disodium phosphate, disodium inosinate and guanylate, beta carotene, silicon dioxide.

Before taking off to steal Laverdure the parrot from Pascal, before turning myself into the protagonist of a burlesque sitcom written by a team of hip, young wolves from the CBC, I binge on cheese sticks. I thrust my sticky and already slightly orange hand into the greasy, open bag, driven by a nervous, mechanical, insatiable hunger. My fingers are smeared, damp with the unpleasant oil and cheese-flavoured powder. Once I eat the whole bag, my hand is breaded, covered with a lumpy, phosphorescent, cheese-flavoured crust.

I need a Coke.

I open the fridge, open a can. Ah! We breathe better when

we give in to dietary fury. According to the nutrition facts table on the bag, I have just ingested 300% of my daily serving of salt. I am slowly turning into the Dead Sea.

* * *

I would retrieve Laverdure the parrot. It would be done quickly and well. I had my plan. An old bird cage from the garage, a ragged black sheet from the back of the grey-painted shed. That was all I would need.

I took off. Unmasked. An overly small cage under my arm, a black sheet in a huge backpack.

I took action.

As discreet as a whale on a beach in Normandy.

Slipping into the night, I sank into a delinquency that helped my digestion, clogged up with cheese-flavoured powder.

Arrived at Pascal's apartment. Legs firmly planted on the ground. Cage deposited on the sidewalk. Back still damp from bearing the heat of the black sheet in my 80 L backpack. Silent, itching to start, like any criminal before committing a crime. But I was no criminal. I was an agent of cultural transmission, working to promote local literature. I repeated this stupid mantra, trying to convince myself that it wasn't stupid. Ever so carefully, I sneaked onto my friend's balcony.

I call Pascal my friend, but he is my rival, in a way. Our interactions follow this relational model: disparaging judgment followed by neglect and vaguely contemptuous scepticism followed by unflattering comments. Be that as it may, Laverdure the parrot was rightfully mine. In the dubious balance of our friendship, it fell to Pascal to be betrayed at least once. I'm not stupid so much as I am puerile.

In an ecstatic vision, I saw myself brandishing a glass cutter in the right hand and the puny cage in the other. An unfortunate apparition, with which I distracted myself for a moment. Distraction.

Then I quickly tucked the cutter back in my pocket and threw the cage off Pascal's balcony with an insolent clang.

There I was, Ghislain the reader, nothing but a common thief.

I would call Pascal in a few hours to explain myself.

PASCAL: Ghislain! What are you doing here?

The noise made by the cage falling and crashing below the balcony had produced results. Pascal came out, scrutinized me from head to toe, annoyed but with a mocking air.

GHISLAIN: Listen, I...

PASCAL: You wake me at this hour to tell me: *Listen, I...* Frankly, voicemail works too.

GHISLAIN: I have to tell you something... the parrot...

PASCAL: The parrot is doing fine. I found a sheet and a cage, and it's sleeping now. Tomorrow, I'll take it to the SPCA.

GHISLAIN: I need it to recruit readers.

PASCAL: What are you talking about?

GHISLAIN: Laverdure the parrot is a sign; it didn't come here by chance. I would like to take it for a few days so I can teach it a few things.

PASCAL: This again! It is not Laverdure the parrot. It's the parrot of an eccentric who taught it a phrase spoken by a parrot in a novel.

GHISLAIN: I'm not asking you to throw yourself into the fire. I'm simply asking you to let me conduct a small experiment.

PASCAL: This parrot isn't yours. You're being ridiculous.

GHISLAIN: No, I'm not being ridiculous.

PASCAL: Yes, you're being ridiculous.

GHISLAIN: No, I'm not being ridiculous.

PASCAL: Yes, you're being ridiculous.

GHISLAIN: I want people to think they're seeing an apparition in 3D. Imagine a parrot saying: "You must read Jean Basile. You must read *Le Grand Khan*," flying all around the city. All of a sudden, people become curious, they wonder: Who is this Jean Basile? What is *Le Grand Khan*?

PASCAL: Everyone will think it's one of Cossette's new ads and give the bird a good kick.

GHISLAIN: If it only works once, then it only works once. But at least I tried!

PASCAL: It's ridiculous.

GHISLAIN: No, it's not ridiculous.

PASCAL: It's ridiculous.

GHISLAIN: No, it's not ridiculous.

PASCAL: Ah, go to sleep!

* * *

To: readmeagain@sympatico.ca
From: earnestoearnesto@gmail.com

Ghislain, what got into you?

3. LAVERDURE THE PARROT

Pascal told me you wanted to steal the parrot and turn it into a marketing agent!

It's pathetic but really cute!

I finished reading *Le Grand Khan*. You make me laugh because Basile is in fact a Russian immigrant... This has no bearing on his novel, which is unilaterally Montrealist and Quebecois, but it's just that I realized that there is no literature *de souche*, no literature of Quebecois origin, that Simon Harel, who wrote a book on "identity poaching," was right... that now we have to steal the part of ourselves that defines us. I don't want to get into an abstruse discussion, but I read about twenty pages of Harel's book. He writes: "In contrast to discourses that euphorically promote the success of dissident forms of cultural hybridity, poaching does not have any meaning in itself. From this perspective, poaching has the virtue of indicating strategies of deterritorialization that transform a place into a dynamic space. The true usefulness of poaching rests in actively promoting the dissolution of territorial control."

A compelling metaphor... an illegal hunt that takes the form of identity brutality, where we take what we want without ever submitting to consensus.

Harel adds: "[Poaching] is a tactic with limited power. Sometimes, it is a cruel practice. In the discomfort that poaching produces... lies a muted violence we must learn to recognize."

For me, *Le Grand Khan* is the story of a poacher, a cultural poacher, conceited and pretentious, egotistical and narcissistic. He kills hope and imposes his writer's life as an identity weapon.

Basile describes some of this in *Le Grand Khan*: "Let us get on with it. Tonight, I want to rule because, for once, it is easy, not like a queen bee over a noisy empire teeming with wings, but over none other than myself, less imperious than Genghis Khan, my intrinsic hordes obeying my smallest command, not exactly proud of being that, but content in knowing how to be that, and drawing joy from this, on this infinitely profound and fresh night, having no one to meet but the unexpected, no more work, no more friends, free as the wind, breathing whatever odours I want, rejecting noises that wear me down, retaining only those that, tonight, delight my well-trained ear, eyes almost closed, falsely blind and walking on brightly lit streets, which henceforth belong to me."

As for me, I would have taught your parrot a few book titles to promote. An adventurous parrot that relentlessly repeated the title of a new book everyday, but in a different part of the city, would be a formidable marketing agent. In any case, you know as well as I do that the number of books to promote vastly exceeds the number of reviewers... This is why I have given myself the task of dazzling you with my research skills. I've just finished reading *Catéchèse** by Patrick Brisebois, a thin novel, a novella if you like, whose voice stands out from the rest of the books being published nowadays... a short

---

* *Catechism*. (Trans.)

3. LAVERDURE THE PARROT

lesbiano-ann-héberto-science-fictional novel... a hybrid work completely of its time. So many old-fashioned books die on the shelves of the Grande Bibliothèque that I can't help but be glad that this author exists. I appreciated the overall quality, the perceptible progression towards science fiction (it capitalizes a bit on the concept of role play in *SimCity*), the gallery of nasty female characters, and the archaic village frozen in time... and I found the part about masturbating with a Virgin Mary figurine pretty funny...

Just between you and me, I agree with you, Laverdure the parrot came to us the other day of its own accord, to sanctify us and stress our quiet apostleship...

Take care!

Courrège

xx

4.

REVERIES OF A DISORIENTED RAMBLER-CLERK

READING HAD GIVEN ME AN OASIS OF CALM, HAD
guided me like an abstract mentor into a comfortable desert.
But recently, it had transformed into a method of persecu-
tion. Yet I didn't ask for much—just to carry out my work,
write my reports, receive my cheques. The story with the parrot cruelly crippled my routine. I could never have imagined
the extent to which a bird would crush me.

I had understood that the life of a reader is that of an as-
saulted rambler.

Why all the effort to resurrect him if not to express the con-
junction of aggression and my predisposed vulnerability; at
least here, there is no danger, cities are angels for those who

know how to nestle under their wings, I will build you a city out of rags, me, passionate about what I do and knowing it like a glove all the way to the fingertips, at my signal, the stone forests and human sea will rise, no longer flowing as it once did, roaring from window to window, eager chrysalis exploding the cocoon, but with calculated slowness, like the marching Royal Guard, step by step, barely grazing the ground, or taking me for Rousseau, collecting plants in the streets, a solitary rambler, finding all the names, the places, to each their duty and their privilege, like a secret route, calm, immobile, permanent, almost consoling.

Page 118 of *Le Grand Khan*, page 675 of my fantasy autobiography.

* * *

"The form of a city changes faster, alas, than the human heart." This is not me, but Jacques Roubaud, as per the two Waldrops, his translators. It's a title. In the style of Queneau or Réda, he gave us, in *The Form of a City Changes Faster, Alas, Than the Human Heart*, childlike snapshots, witticisms husked in an urban recycling bin.

This morning, I set out on the streets of Montreal in search of words abandoned on the road, sheets of paper, taking myself for Roubaud. It's soothing to settle oneself in an imagined body and to manoeuvre this body with a driver's confidence.

I strolled in Parc Saint-Émile. Its cracked sidewalks and decrepit benches gave me the impression that the park was turning into an artifact. I stopped for a few moments by the pétanque field, a gravel court enclosed in a narrow wooden frame at most fifteen centimetres high. The place was deserted, no pétanque players in sight. I went on my way.

On the other side of the street, a few bits of paper were stuck to the sidewalk. I crossed the street. The sun had not yet drained all the moisture from these dead fibres.

First, I found a lined sheet, folded into an awkward accordion by the foul weather. It was someone's homework, part of an essay. A grade was written in the upper right corner, a few red marks on the page. It was an exam. The person who had written the essay had left an empty space between each line of writing to give the teacher room to indicate what didn't work, what was wrong, what would have to be thrown out.

The teacher had not been severe. The essay still had some small errors and two or three inappropriate, badly chosen words left unmarked.

In my own way, I, too, was an anonymous, even hidden, teacher. Instead of covering the manuscripts I received with red scrawl, I held back, kept to the sidelines, left to others the thankless task of transmitting to my victims the essence of my reservations and rejections.

I was nameless, faceless. I was Ghislain the reader to my friends, if they felt like harmlessly teasing me, but otherwise, to all the others, I was Ghislain the anonymous.

I had the job of a hypocrite. I wouldn't have been able to say if I was among the most competent ones in the field, but I carried out my task with all the professionalism that it demanded.

I wanted to choose good books. I wanted to control people, at my own pace, millimetre by millimetre, title by title, by injecting a dose of my tastes, which I believed to be sound, into the publishing program of a publishing house I admired.

I had wanted to be part of a certain editorial continuity. So, at that point, I was feeling a bit disoriented.

I crumpled the essay and threw it, like a pétanque ball, to the other side of the street. It didn't quite reach the pétanque field.

A bit farther off, near the corner of Rachel and Saint-Germain, I spotted another paper ball. Much more compact, the size of a large marble. Carefully, I started to smooth it out. It was a sheet torn out of a cash receipt book, Classic brand. In the lower left corner, a "thank you" was printed in cursive letters to compensate for the potential lack of etiquette of waiters or clerks.

I strolled around like an affectionate dilettante, a solitary dreamer, noticing the abundance of written materials.

Even though I loved with an epic passion the unaffected lucidity of Laurent-Michel Vacher, our most frank and determined Quebecois atheist materialist, I was first and foremost a literary man. That is to say, a pseudo theologian of writing.

Every reader is a disappointed Platonist, in search of time.

The literature that is most objective and least polite in its surprising rawness, its frankness, always accepts the world of ideas, the world of forms. It's impossible to escape it. Every reader of fiction is either an awkward idealist or an oblivious idealist. We cannot escape it.

The human being is made of perishable material that, for a moment before dying, thinks. This transition that leads us to death, in whatever way we experience it, is filled with ideas we gather from books, just like me today gathering these unimportant scraps strewn across the street after the rain.

Already knowing he was condemned, Vacher wrote brilliantly about the difficult subject of death in his *Carnet devant la mort*.* Page after page, he states his atheist credo, at all times trying to escape the ghosts of literature, of philosophy—that coquette in a dressing gown—to flee the elegant turns of phrase that only result in affectation or a convenient confusion intended to factitiously increase the writing's profound depth (a term that he actually ridicules, rejecting the nobleness we usually give it). He writes:

> I belong to a living species, the Homo sapiens sapiens as the experts call it. From what they say, as I intimated at the beginning, there are over six billion of these speaking primates on the planet—a figure that, frankly, seems unimaginable. To somehow comprehend its concrete meaning, I try never to lose sight of the fact that every minute this translates into roughly 100 deaths (approximately 1.66 per second) and 260 births (4.33 per second)! I thus imagine a giant screen, like in an IMAX theatre, with six billion small flickering lights, with an entry zone in the upper left side and an exit in the lower right, where every second we could see the 4.33 sparks of newborn life appear and the 1.66 sparks die out and disappear.
>
> I do not know if many of our brains would be able to endure such a spectacle. Instead, I bet that my fellow creatures and I would only morally survive if we forgot these figures, vertiginous and inhuman to us, of which an overly clear awareness would trivialize our usual sense of importance to such an extent that it would feel almost unbearable, not to

---

* Vacher's *Une petite fin du monde: Carnet devant la mort* [A Small End of the World: Notebook Before Death] was published by Éditions Liber in 2005. (Trans.)

mention the possible damage done to our encouraging ethical respect for all human life... (Stalin: "The death of one man is a tragedy. The deaths of millions is a statistic.")

In any event, we can therefore say that in terms of abstract knowledge, we now know the lottery of life and death with a fairly high degree of objective precision, but we have not been adequately equipped (through natural evolution or divine will, it's of little import here) to intuitively cope with it without having to pay a seemingly too high a price.

Pages 60 and 61 of *Une petite fin du monde: Carnet devant la mort*, page 710 of my imaginary confessions.

* * *

There.

I punch the large metal plate. The blue handicap button vibrates for a moment. The sliding door lets me pass.

I go into the Grande Bibliothèque, my sanctuary, my oasis.

I give a confidential nod to the Swahili warrior with authoritative braids guarding the entrance of the great Montreal Sphinx, then pass the magnetic arches, the green signs, and then, the still staircase. I head for the elevator. If one were to see a progression in the events that follow, that would be a mistake, because everything happens all at once; I forget all about Basile, Maldonne, and Pascal for sixty-eight seconds.

Suddenly, Patrick Poulin's sweet voice resounds: "Congratulations! You have just won a set of systems!" (*Morts de Low Bat*, Le Quartanier, 2007.)

In the elevator, a man in his sixties takes me in his arms and whispers: "I am Laverdure the parrot." It was him. A man in his sixties, going up to the fourth floor of the large book complex.

An ascent towards the moving image and orchestrated sounds.

He tells me: "Chatter, chatter."

I chattered, and for good reason! I was a first-rate chatterbox.

Then he holds out his hand, the way you hold out your hand to a second-zone being, a bit contemptuous with extreme Royal Academy haughtiness.

Then he says: "That's all you ever do, and how unfortunate for you."

Waiting for my hands to reach my mouth, tell my eyes and then my brain that words are required.

Waiting, therefore, for articulated language to arise, I nervously stop in my tracks.

A film crew, directed by Louis Malle, has taken the opportunity to infiltrate the building, in order to handle my characteristic lack of reaction. What those in the field call the "Marceline effect." They install a plank on wheels under my feet, fitted with a small, silent motor, remote-controlled to move an actor standing upright, impassive. I am like a stork on a scaffold. Everything stirs around me while I move with renewed confidence.

So I am rolling between the stacks on the second floor at the pace imposed by the grips of the camera crew. Moving quickly, head still, the unusual set scrolling by. They film me from below, from the side, under the buttocks, a Trojan Horse on wheels.

Calmly, feeling a trace of faint love for the human race (though my perspective has changed somewhat since reading

Vacher: "I do believe that I will leave this world convinced that Christians are mistaken: 'to love your neighbour' is at best an illusion, at worst a potentially destructive force. I'll take the rule of law and justice a hundred times over." *Une petite fin du monde: Carnet devant la mort*), I grab one of Gallimard's "Quarto" books, *Moi et mon double*, a volume of selected writing by Gombrowicz.

Nothing is ever trivial in choosing a book.

Opening it, I notice an ex libris—an unexpected label in a book intended for the collective masses. After scanning the bookplate for a second and third time, I realize that it's an artwork. I read:

> A part of you on this book—Sep 29, 1998. The fingerprints found on the cover of this book were collected. These fingerprints were then carefully analyzed at the Centre des arts actuels Skol during the winter of 1999. The results of this research now belong to you. Some of the samples collected were presented in a display case in the hall of the Main Library, near the circulation desk. The rest of the work is being conserved as part of a controlled humidity and temperature reserve collection.

This is ex libris number 84.

On the left side of the bookplate, a justified text provides further information about the artist's project: "Everywhere, on every book of this library, you leave your fingerprints over those of the previous readers. Together with the others, you form a skin on every work without realizing it."

And written in small lettering on the lower left: "A project by Raphaëlle de Groot."

Then, the book's call number on the right: 891.8537 G 632 mo.

I forget about Courrège.

Laverdure the parrot says: "Chatter, chatter, it's a problem."

Laverdure the parrot says: "Chatter, chatter, you're always the problem, chatter, that's all."

So I will be the problem and that will be all.

* * *

To: readmeagain@sympatico.ca
From: earnestoearnesto@gmail.com

Ghighi!

You're still depressed!

You wander! You see ghosts!

My colleagues told me that you were pacing up and down the second floor of the G.B. Were you looking for me? Let's see a movie or grab a meal soon... whenever you like... Pick up the phone!

Later!
Courrège
xx

5.

C LIKE CINEMA

MALDONNE WAS MILKING HIM. SIPHONING HIM, SUCKING him off, getting her fill. A persistent and experienced farmer, she nodded in agreement, barely swayed through salivary noises, plunged back into apnea, her glottis getting hammered.

Sex overflowed at Pascal's place. Maldonne flailed in his bed, writhed like a Desdemona, swallowed with tenderness. Over 300 million unborn North Americans downloaded into the moist environment and swam. Pascal stopped puffing and panting; he'd shot his load.

Then, hands. One pair of hands, another pair of hands. Twisting and kneading, Pascal confirmed the presence of

Maldonne's breasts. An anatomy lesson on a nighttime divan, "yes" repeated faster and faster until the final YES.

Well, not exactly a nighttime divan, but a Louis IV sofa.

Fucking is a less conventional art than farting, but as reassuring as walking.

We had to come together, before the pre-Viagra panic and andropause, on the field of unmade beds and pornographic citations.

Groan, and you frown; spit out, and geese come out; do the nasty, your hair gets messy; lash out, and they put out.

* * *

I open the door and say "hello."

I'm getting manuscripts. It's nice outside. A sunny, blue sky. I walk to the back of the office, pull on the handle of the metal cabinet.

In the shadows, there are packs of paper, boxes of paper-clips, manila envelopes, rolls of fax paper, jars of rubber bands, scissors, piles of bubble envelopes, binder clips of different sizes heaped on a tray.

I rummage and poke around, for the sole pleasure of rummaging and poking around. It passes the time. Then I make a deft turn on my left foot. I become a reader that notes and compiles once more.

Bergamote hands me the bag of four manuscripts. Four more sanitary tasks, four more verdicts to decide.

Bergamote skims the reader reports I've brought her. The papers rustle in her hands, her decision is made before she's reached the bottom of the page.

While she's busy examining my reading notes, I scan the

titles of the new manuscripts she's given me: *Melancholic Passion* by Jean-Michel Arvasti (no doubt a heavy-handed political thriller); *The Shack That Struck* by Ginette Falardeau (a memoir or a fantasy crime novel with a rural tang of the mall art gallery variety, although the title is not uninteresting, vaguely intriguing, already a good point); *Censorship in Marieville* by Sébastien Ducharme (a moral-political rant with severe acne, or an amateur whodunit with asinine moralizing, the title doesn't bode well); *The Golgotha of Tears* by Fabrice LeBreton (ugh! an edifying Melgibsonian work or a maudlin pensum, written with excessive compassion, it's hard to expect anything other than a literary disaster: title in bad taste, metaphorical immoderation, inane imagination—I already have my reasons for rejecting it, now I just have to confirm my disgust...).

Bergamote has finished reading. She raises her head. A few minutes have passed. She tells me: "So nothing good, in the end."

I tell her: "A bad batch."

Easygoing about the routine, Bergamote deposits the now officially rejected manuscripts on a pile under her desk. She unsticks the "REJECTED" Post-it note from the previous top manuscript in the pile and sticks it on the new manuscript that has just joined its lost companions.

The cycle continues.

My mission: show no mercy.

My life is a bad novel I had the decency not to write. My distribution neurosis compensates for all the asceticism.

* * *

Maldonne is nibbling on some buttered toast. Pascal serves her coffee. A moment of respite.

MALDONNE: Delicious.

PASCAL: More butter?

MALDONNE: No, I'm fine.

PASCAL: How do you take your coffee?

MALDONNE: Black.

PASCAL: Want a biscotti?

MALDONNE: No, thanks.

Some time passes.

PASCAL: I haven't heard any news about the parrot. I imagine its owner picked it up.

MALDONNE: Or some enthusiast bought it...

PASCAL: Perhaps it's already roasted...

MALDONNE: A chicken deluxe!

PASCAL: A dinner with feathers!

MALDONNE: "Boo!... Boo!..." It's Laverdure the parrot! (*Stereotypical ghostly movements, mouth like a hen's arse.*)

PASCAL: Booooo!... Litterrrratuuuuuurre pays us a visit... Fiction suddenly looms up in reality... (*Exaggerated pronunciation, Yves P. Pelletier comic effect.*)

MALDONNE (*chuckling*): Poor Ghislain.

PASCAL: Poor asshole, yes. He needs to get a real job.

MALDONNE: He's not an asshole, just a bit nutso, depressed.

PASCAL: Okay, you have fifteen seconds to think of as many depressives as you can among our common friends... Go!

Fifteen seconds pass.

MALDONNE: Shit, I thought of ten!

PASCAL: Go ahead, name them!

MALDONNE: Ghislain (goes without saying), Marco Bédard, Isabelle Lavigne, Jean-François Beauregard, Émile-Sacha

Dovari, Chantal Gariépy, Manolo Carrière, Stéphane Sicotte, Viviane Norah, Emmanuel Landry. It's ridiculous.

PASCAL: If everyone's sick, then it's no longer a sickness.

MALDONNE: So what is it?

PASCAL: A new human state. A stronger form of melancholy. In the past, drinking used to be enough.

MALDONNE: It's sad, all this. Poor Ghislain.

PASCAL: He'll come back from his parrot. Naïveté is not incurable, you know.

MALDONNE: It's him I'm worried about, not his parrot.

Pascal awkwardly makes himself a cappuccino.

MALDONNE: He needs a girlfriend. Or someone to persuade.

PASCAL: Ghislain's definitely heavy-handed. The problem is that he imposes his anxieties on us, as if we needed them. The other night, I felt like I was talking to a depressed politician who'd lost his grip.

MALDONNE: What's he done to you that you're bitching about him like this? He just needs some help, like everyone else.

PASCAL: He needs a shrink.

MALDONNE: It's not as bad as that. He just needs a nice girl. He's like a baby. You need to give him lots of attention, coddle him a bit, listen to him. I like reading too, but I'm not caught up in his religion... When it comes down to it, Ghislain is a sectarian, a Jehovah's Witness of the Quebecois book.

PASCAL: I can just see him with a suitcase full of books, going door to door, summarizing the plots, offering...

MALDONNE: He wouldn't sink as much into his neurosis if a chick pulled him out of the hole when needed.

PASCAL: Listen, I like Ghislain just fine, but in my opinion,

he needs a decent salary, good entertainment, travel. And a
clear diagnosis to know what pills to take.

MALDONNE: No, I'm telling you, he just needs a chick...

PASCAL: Forget it. A chick with that much patience doesn't
come with the "Books" supplement in the *Devoir*...

MALDONNE: It's possible.

PASCAL: Everything is possible. Even Laverdure the parrot!
In a fantasy world, guys like Ghislain are married to beautiful
princesses and busy with their court of elfish minions carrying chestnut-stuffed pheasants on silver trays, and drinking
"heady" wines in crystal goblets (*trying to look like a dimwit*).

*　*　*

How will I be remembered? How will people remember me?

10:57 p.m.

There's a lineup at the cash. Always the same lineup before
11 p.m. I'm working alone in this fucking dep, and everyone
comes to buy what everyone comes to buy a few minutes
before 11 p.m. Tastes are varied, the choice is varied. A twelve-
pack of Budweiser, one Fin du monde, a vodka cooler, two
brown Boréale, a six-pack of Heineken in cans, a large bottle
of Black Label, a large bottle of Red Bull, a twelve-pack of
Wildcat. Eight people in line and more coming through the
door, already beating a path to the fridges. I hurry. Take out
my key. Enforce the law. I have eight doors to lock, eight beer
caves to seal off. Behind the counter earlier, I managed to roll
down the screen over the wine section. Not very popular. I
get it. Beer is the quality alcohol in deps. As quickly as possible, before the impatient rabble gets a chance to lose their
cool, I turn the small key to the right in all the locks of the

alcohol fridges. I've become an expert. Complete the proce-
dure in under thirty seconds. Then quickly get back behind
the till. It's a mess. There are some administrative tasks to finish, paperwork to fill out. It's all piled up on my Loto-Québec
counter-top display. I hide all of the varieties of scratch & win
cards and lotto tickets. Avoid thinking about two or three
customers. Two or three customers that I often see a few
minutes before 11 p.m. and around noon, when I work days.

The 11 p.m. rush is over.

That's it. By the end of the night, I will have to refuse to
sell beer to at least three people. At least one drunk per week
always comes to the counter to drool for beer. Even if they
are ready to pay me, I have to enforce the law, and I enforce
it. Between 11 p.m. and the early morning hours, there's no
longer a means of escaping reality through alcohol. You must
be stocked up in advance or resort to other substances.

How will I be remembered?

A young woman, no more than twenty-five, comes in to
fuel up on slush. She fills a medium-sized cup (way too enormous for my stomach) with slush the colour of fresh blood.
A fluorescent crimson mixture, cherry flavoured.

The same stupid question seems rooted to the spot, on the
other side of the counter, like the nighttime customers, the
thirsty zombies of modern times.

I don't blame them, I don't judge them. I don't care. I enforce the law, squeezed into my uniform that comes down to
a blue shirt. If I had a gun, I would be a soldier or a policeman;
if I wore white, I would be an administrator, doctor or nurse,
a cook or a barber; if I wore an orange jumpsuit, I would be a
prisoner. The uniform reassures people. It reinforces prejudices and helps people avoid total confusion. It's a con job

and an identity barrier all at once. Even though the uniform has much less prestige today than it once did, it remains a convenient bastion against the onslaught of madness.

How will my time on earth be remembered?

A pack of Belvedere Extra Mild and a pack of Excel Extreme Shock gum. A clean, bearded man in a trendy windbreaker.

How will I be remembered?

As part of the silent majority, a shadow: *Je suis une ombre.*

Two jittery youths come in. I watch them but don't really give a damn, either. They return with a bag of black pepper and jack cheese Doritos and two litres of Coke Zero. The more nervous of the two also buys a Mr. Big and a pack of Craven "A" cigarettes. He looks to be about eighteen—no zeal tonight. They pay and leave.

How will we be remembered?

I recall reading an article on this topic by Stanley Péan in an issue of *Alibis* (a clone of American crime magazines, same format, same layout, same questionable graphic design).

Péan had written something along the lines of—I'm quoting from memory: "In the future, people will say about the people of our era: they read newspapers and watched TV."

So, for some future historians, we would become newspaper readers and couch potatoes.

Would I not then be a typical, authentic product, a characteristic human of my era? Me, Ghislain the reader.

A bag of ketchup-flavoured Lay's, a carton of Québon chocolate milk. The young woman pays without even looking at me. She's preoccupied with something else.

Will people remember that those like me helped shape our era?

Not necessarily. Those who write will end up in archives and on library shelves, gaining stature day by day.

That said, more adventurous researchers will perhaps unearth piles of reading reports left behind by the readers of publishing houses, if those houses give their archives to the Bibliothèque nationale du Québec or Library and Archives Canada. A few years ago, the reading reports of Georges Perros, a reader for *La Nouvelle Revue Française* and the Théâtre National de Paris, were published.

A large bar of Poulain chocolate. The customer, with a melancholic air, stares wearily at my hands with increasing effort—he definitely needs his sugar fix.

What will people remember about me?

Nothing, no doubt. And I don't even care that much, in fact. Perros, in any case, doesn't count. He was first and foremost a poet, a writer. Someone more generous than me, who had the clarity to title one of his books *Une vie ordinaire.** Of all his work, this one is surely what will live on. The freshness of truth never gets old.

As for me, my friends will bury me, still believing the prejudices they already have against me, the envy and contempt they don't dare articulate.

With respect to history with a capital I I, we are all convenience store customers after eleven at night, stooping shadows, unable to reconsider our habits and take our normal, healthy human comfort into account. Silhouettes with no courage, no audacity, no constructive ambition. (Everywhere, narcissism and destruction reign supreme.)

---

* *An Ordinary Life.* (Trans.)

I am a normal, healthy human being. I am Ghislain the reader. If I don't write anything about the appearance of Laverdure the parrot, no one will know anything about it. Since I will not write anything about Laverdure the parrot, no one will hear anything about Ghislain the reader. I don't give a damn.

In a way, I'm protecting myself from future disappointment.

Every normal individual over thirty has constructed their identity based on one or two well-kept secrets. The theory of *My New Partner* (a film by Claude Zidi that hasn't aged well), that each one of us has something to feel guilty about, is not entirely true. It would have been more apt to say that each one of us *either has* something to feel guilty about *or invents* something to feel guilty about. A nuance, therefore. In both cases, there's a secret. Everyone needs a secret. It's the only way to make ourselves interesting to the majority. Our identity is based on a secret, or two or three at best. So when we meet perceptive people who see through us, we feel as though we're standing naked before them, emptied of our content. And rarely is there much content. Depth is a mere three or four paragraphs behind a mysterious assertion, that's all. The rest is marginalia. It gives work to so-called intellectuals. I am not an intellectual, I am a reader. It's different. However, I must admit that everyone's secrets give me work. No secrets means no manuscripts, no desire to disclose oneself, or to refuse to disclose oneself by beating about the bush for fifty attempts at a novel.

A jar of Cheez Whiz, a litre of 1% milk, a loaf of Weston whole wheat bread, and a copy of *People*. The man smiles at me. He's sporting a black leather jacket, a nose ring, and a tattoo on his neck ("More Skull"), all consistent with the neighbourhood stereotype. The man chooses 1% milk. He is someone who reads, no doubt. He is also someone who plays with his secret.

* * *

To: readmeagain@sympatico.ca
From: earnestoearnesto@gmail.com

Hey Caveboy!

Are we going to the movies?

I'm still going to be your friend, even if you don't call me anymore.

I've been looking through the film listings in the papers... on *Rotten Tomatoes* and IMBD... I keep finding interesting things (that's the theme: interesting things). You know, it's like the Americans say: "...like a kid in a candy store." Well, now I'm the one in front of all these movies that are making me drool.

Should we pick something at random? I'll give you three choices: a film at random; a film playing at a specific time on a specific day; a flop.

Does that work for you? Tell me what you think...

Cut out the letters of the alphabet and put them in a small envelope! Then if you pick the letter Q, for example, I suggest *The Queen* by Stephen Frears (Dianesque times, Elizabeth II played by a flawless actress, a director at the peak of his career, fiction bordering on documentary with a particularly attentive art director...) If you pick the letter B, we'll see *Babel* by Iñárritu, who directed *Amores Perros* and *21 Grams* (a virtuosic interweaving of stories like his previous films, Brad Pitt and Cate Blanchett in the main roles, story of language, nightmare of Babel, unbearable suspense and drama... have I piqued your interest?). For letter C, we have *Congorama* by our old favourite, Philippe Falardeau (did well at Cannes, features an emu (a kind of ostrich), Paul Ahmarani and Olivier Gourmet (awesome actor and a favourite of the Dardenne brothers), sociological look at regional Quebec with a plot twist, good reviews).

Shall I go on?

Two more letters... If you feel like a flop, it's easier, you don't need any letters, just pick a genre... that will determine the type of flop: horror equals a bloody flop, a series of successful and unsuccessful special effects; adolescent comedy equals a good flop, if the amount of scatological, sexual, contemptuous, jackass, and sadistic jokes exceeds the amount of good feelings and moral twists; a war or sports movie equals an excellent flop, if the amount of courage and psychological and physical obstacles, as well as the rate of action scenes, scenes of slaughter or difficult surgeries (amputating, sewing up organs, sawing off parts of the skull) exceed the sentimental parts in which people socialize, touch each other, share their fears, and talk about their childhoods.

Relying on a formula either means we lack imagination or implies the necessity of a movie package intended for a target audience that wants a particular set of images, sounds, actors, story lines... Our choices are horror, adolescent comedy, sentimental comedy, dramatic comedy, educational animation, drama, historical film, war movie, sports flick, superslow activist documentary (those that go beyond ideology are interesting)... There are many types of flops. In any case, this represents 84% of the movies now showing.

Another letter?

If you give me D, I propose Scorsese's *The Departed*, a remake of an Asian film, since the best action films now come out of Asia (DiCaprio, Nicholson, Damon, tons of intrigue and serious dialogue, a mole within the police, a rat with the mafiosi, Boston, duel between DiCaprio and Damon, choreographed, naturalistic violence, the Scorsese touch—domineering masculinity with no safe conduct, moral conflict and Christian redemption in a dirty rotten world, the indecent brutality of life in the underworld).

Last one: S, *The Science of Sleep* by Michel Gondry (because it stars Charlotte Gainsbourg, because Gondry is an inventive director of music videos, because he directed *Eternal Sunshine of the Spotless Mind*, because he's an exhilarating post-surrealist, the offspring of Orson Welles and Terry Gilliam, an aesthete still enamoured with the cadaverous beauty of cinema, the opulence of the complex frame). Alright? Shall we decide?

Seriously, I can be patient, but only up to a point... I'll give you two days to decide.

Courrège
xx

6.

THE GUYAUDIAN

BEING DISGUISED. NEEDING TO BE DISGUISED. TO SLIP by unnoticed, run through the streets, mount a campaign, dive into the flow. A seasonal necessity, a pretext for plastic junk and industrial sugar. It was Halloween. A common celebration. In the future, once borders between countries disappear and only one central government representing the human race circulates goods and services in the hope that it will function like an automaton of justice, programmed like a paterfamilias for all its children, we will begin to think. We will realize that life is an ordeal we must tend to until death.

Meditating and moaning, going through hell and understanding.

Our whole life, we must suffer the suffering eyes of the multitude; catch the contemptuous or indifferent eyes of our fellow beings, our whole life; think we're making a difference here, when, at the same time, everything lies in poverty there; devise utopias for our own sake, to put our minds at ease; taste poverty ourselves in a world of plenty, our whole life, see the need for frugality, for our ability to survive under the weight of our imperial, predatory foolishness, our whole life; and die in intense psychological pain, in ordinary solitude, borne by the courage of atheists.

Halloween was a time to ponder these questions, to get out of bed trembling with fear, contemplating the answers to these questions. Halloween was a seasonal illness, an amusing way to die all together.

In *ICI* (a weekly published by Quebecor), "just for fun" Michel Vézina asked the readers of his blog (today, anyone without a blog is just not an interesting human being): "Without cheating, how many of you could name five Quebecois novelists?" It was an innocent question, a curious challenge. Of their own accord, Quebec literary critics, of which Vézina is one, are rather pessimistic and tend to underestimate the knowledge of the general public. Despite the digital selectivity (a question asked on a little-read blog) that always cuts us off from at least 70% of the population (illiteracy, poverty, primary school education, and overwhelming lack of interest in the thing) and always calls upon the same 20% of citizens who are literate and online (post-secondary education, engagement, reading, general knowledge and desire to write), Vézina hit a wall: most of the top 20% knew at least five Quebecois novelists. I quote:

6. THE GUYAUDIAN

Comment by Amélie Bernard: Not too difficult... Patrick Senécal, Julie Hivon, Maxime-Olivier Moutier, Matthieu Simard, Marie-Sissi Labrèche, Natasha Beaulieu, Jean-Jacques Pelletier, Mélika Abdelmoumen... And cheating a bit (by looking at my own bookshelves): Gaétan Soucy, Bruno Hébert, Jacques Côté, Robert Malacci, Joël Champetier, Jacques Bissonnette. All authors read, often reread, and often several books by each.

There's no doubt, this commentator is part of the upper echelon of the 20%. An avid reader who likes books published by Alire, a consumer of genre fiction (fantasy, horror) who keeps up to date, reads newspapers, is on the lookout for literary news. If she's not a university graduate, she's an autodidact who is curious and doesn't need a credit rating to define her life. If all of *ICI*'s readers were as eclectic and informed, we would (almost) be living in an ideal world. *Ergo problema.* So let us, light-heartedly, consider this reader the exception.

Comment by Red Panda: Guillaume Vigneault, Chrystine Brouillet, Anne Hébert, Victor-Lévy Beaulieu, François Avard, Jacques Poulin, Jacques Godbout, Germaine Guèvremont, Francine Ruel... And many others, some even better, who have slipped my mind at the moment.

Panda names a compendium of authors taught in college or authors who appear in print media and especially on TV. Panda has no doubt graduated from college, maybe even university, watches TV, knows authors that make a splash, has popular but also literary tastes (these are not mutually exclusive). She is a diligent reader who likes the stars of Quebec fiction. She is undoubtedly politically engaged. She is at least thirty years old and comes from Montreal.

Comment by Johanne Sauvé: No one has mentioned Michel Tremblay; still, he's one of the most well-known! There's also Mark Fisher, Marthe Gagnon-Thibaudeau, Yves Beauchemin, Marie-Claire Blais, Charlotte Boisjoli and Leonard Cohen, to name just a few.

Johanne is part of the segment of readers born in the forties or fifties. Speaking up for Michel Tremblay is their right. Johanne is also a diligent reader, has not studied literature but appreciates good, fat books, historical sagas, sentimental novels. She is attracted to bestsellers: by mentioning Mark Fisher in her choice of authors, she admits being moved by enticing books like *The Instant Millionaire* or *The Golfer and the Millionaire*. Fisher's goal: to show you how to become a millionaire by writing books, just like him, that will be translated into many languages. He uses a narrative technique that he will teach you for the modest sum of $300 at one of his weekend workshops and lectures. Dubious, but the man has all the arguments of popular success on his side. Under these conditions, it's difficult to redirect the general public towards *Le Grand Khan* (incompatible greatnesses). Too underground, doesn't consider his readers, writes in long sentences, no action. Doesn't give his readers what they want. Mark Fisher is the archenemy of difficult books, the nemesis of all Jean Basiles.

Question: How many manuscripts written by Fisher's disciples have I rejected in my line of work? Answer: Many.

So what did I learn by reading this blog? That readers remember the names of authors who make the news and appear in the media more easily. Okay. That most readers of Quebec novels are women (all three comments were made by women). Cliché. That out of the thirty authors mentioned spontaneously, nineteen are men and eleven are women. Surprising. That no one mentioned Jean Basile. Obvious. That no one remembered a novelist who was also a poet, except for Marie-Claire Blais. Normal. That most of the authors mentioned have published a book in the last five years [less than six out of thirty haven't given a manuscript to their publisher in ages, unless they're well and truly dead (Anne Hébert, Germaine Guèvremont)]. Realistic. And that to try to put Jean Basile's name into circulation, we would need to find a contemporary novelist who would deign to talk about him or transform him into the subject of a novel. That the target audience would ideally be women.

Unlikely scenario.

* * *

Courrège and I at the movies. The operation was successful.

At the Paramount, the huge blue and yellow coil runs down the corner edge of the building. Sainte Catherine Street is aswarm, everywhere: in the underground tunnels, the HMV, the Simons clothing store, and the endless sidewalks.

I stroke her neck. She squeezes my hand. I hug her briefly, she pats my shoulder, our friendship stealthily rushes in beneath the surface, despite ourselves. We play brother and sister.

We've settled on *The Departed* by Scorsese.

I get myself a huge bag of popcorn, Courrège will dip into

it. I sprinkle it with a mix of flavours. I have a method, work at it in steps. First I sprinkle a vibrant orange layer of all-dressed flavour on top, then carefully shake the bag. When the colour has disappeared from the surface, I apply a second layer of white cheese flavour, shake the bag again, then finish with either a layer of barbecue flavour (also orange) or a (red) layer of ketchup flavour. The idea is to equally distribute the flavours in the bag, season every kernel of popcorn, spread the salt and artificial flavours as equally as possible. The most satisfying aspect of this method is that the popcorn never tastes the same a second time, thus giving me the sense that my taste buds never get bored. Scorsese is himself a mixture of several flavours.

Courrège and I have been attending Mass at the cinema for a few years. I sit right next to her, and we slip into the quiet couple–type.

We're at the movies and, naturally, the film is about false-hood.

A ballet of choreographed violence, bird's-eye view of stair-wells, ambiguity, hatred, Irish Catholics, Boston police, cor-rupt emissaries of the Chinese government. Betrayal repaid with betrayal. Gunfire, blood, ass-kicking, a woman caught in the middle, a woman on the side.

The three protagonists die at the end. A convention turned inside out like a glove is still a convention. But the moral is safe, since falsehood is punished.

At the end, when we see Mark Wahlberg's feet wrapped in anti-blood boot covers, we understand that this is not an amoral film, that truth will triumph, that scumbags will bite the dust and pay for their mistakes. Matt Damon will drink from the cup of sincerity at last.

Courrège and I leave a bit before the credits end. There's nothing worse than trying to squeeze between people to get out, even though the audience is small (the end of film in theatres). Yet even these few people exasperate us a little. The experience of the darkness evokes our most philosophical individualism, and few people respect this spontaneous meditative state.

We also find it hard to admit that the cinema is an instrument of false happiness (the power of representation). We want to forget. We try to forget every day, every minute, every second. Psychologists say that we think about sex every seven seconds, so it wouldn't be surprising to learn that we have a cinematographic fantasy every sixty seconds (often of a sexual nature). This is happiness, happiness works in 35 mm and in high-definition video. Ideally, happiness includes many sexual acrobatics, many violent scenes, much bloodshed, many crises of flagrant individualism and megalomaniacal episodes. We invent thousands of scenarios that always come down to a variation on the theme of "I am me!" or "Who am I?" We agonize over getting our turn to speak, and we become ourselves once more when kissing a woman for the first time.

Five minutes of silence, the sacred buffer of post-cinematic decanting. To allow our impressions to settle. Give the post-Scorsese excitement time to diminish and pass. Five minutes, it usually doesn't take more than five minutes of normal, ordinary time. To get up from our seats, leave the theatre, gradually get accustomed to the light—five minutes to come down from the long train of fantasies, the therapeutic session of compensatory bloodshed. We also need time to disconnect from our process of natural identification. We think the film is good if we have identified with it, shared moments with the hero or one of the main characters, and we need to give up this emotional impression of having experienced the action along with the protagonists. Our bodies return to reality in five minutes. No more, no less. In any event, the process is never instantaneous.

After the statutory five minutes, I decided to chat about the film with Courrège. But I was more interested in the questions the film posed than in the film itself. I was bored with the "deceptive" impression that the police and the bad guys are interchangeable and that it's very difficult to discover who is betraying us. The idea that falsehood and contempt do not have a particular physiognomy for Scorsese annoyed me. For me, the question of falsehood had become essential.

* * *

COURRÈGE: *The Departed* is a film about falsehood.

GHISLAIN: Definitely!

COURRÈGE: A moral film about falsehood.

GHISLAIN: Scorsese is always moralistic. The bad guys are punished.

COURRÈGE: Yes, but it's more torturous and sadistic than a normal film.

GHISLAIN: Scorsese is a perverse moralist. He revels in the hyperrealist spectacle of macho violence. He examines the relationships between the dominant and the weak. He loves portraying hierarchies and coded contexts. In this, he is a European director. A Europeanized American.

COURRÈGE: But to get back to the question of falsehood in cinema...

GHISLAIN: We must first consider what falsehood actually is. What does it mean?

COURRÈGE: So what does falsehood actually mean?

GHISLAIN: Well.

COURRÈGE: I feel like I'm in one of Plato's dialogues.

Ghislain is thinking.

COURRÈGE: My name could be Courrègoras or Courrèganaximander!

GHISLAIN: I want to answer you with an aphorism.

COURRÈGE: Okay give me an aphorism.

GHISLAIN: Falsehood is a fantasy pretending to be reality.

COURRÈGE: Wow, that's really clear.

GHISLAIN: But I think it is perfectly clear.

COURRÈGE: Explain it to me in steps... Let's say three steps, like a syllogism. If it's too long, I retain the right to get impatient.

GHISLAIN: I'll use the perspective of a paranoiac to explain falsehood. All cinephiles and moviegoers become, for the duration of a film, paranoiacs in front of the screen... Though, perhaps I'm skipping a step.

COURRÈGE: No doubt more than one, but go on.

GHISLAIN: Okay, listen. Reality is the obvious, the evident. We consider the evident as truth. The evident is true and falsehood distorts truth. Up to this point, we can agree: falsehood distorts the evident.

COURRÈGE: Yes, okay, that works.

GHISLAIN: I'll go on. The sum of all evidence forms the fabric of truth that we could call reality. We cannot consider that which is not evident as real or even as something that can be measured or conceptualized. It's therefore logical to add all known evidence in order to form the totality of what we conveniently call reality. In itself, reality is the sum of all evidence. Everything else belongs to the speculative, the hypothetical, or the mysterious. To this sum of all evidence, I want to add one last evident fact: reality is not based on evidence alone. But, for the moment, let's stick to this basic proposition: reality is the sum of all evidence.

COURRÈGE: Okay, fine. Does it bother you if I eat while I listen.

GHISLAIN: No, listen, it's very simple. Falsehood is a breach in reality, a denial of its evidence. For example, to use Scorsese's elements: a policeman cannot be a policeman; a gangster cannot be a gangster. Analyzing the problem differently leads to a kind of paradox: falsehood does not accept the principle of non-contradiction. So, who are the people who are policemen without being policemen, gangsters without being gangsters? Only one solution solves the problem: we introduce contradictions. Falsehood is based on this about-face, this suspension of the principle of non-contradiction.

COURRÈGE: And fantasy, where does it come in?

GHISLAIN: Fantasy, yes, I've actually just invoked this fearsome fantasy: it's the principle of non-contradiction. To live in accordance with this principle is to condemn oneself to fantasizing reality. At this point, I can reformulate my maxim. Falsehood transforms fantasy into reality.

COURRÈGE: But you've just said that reality stems from the evident?

GHISLAIN: Wait.

COURRÈGE: I'm waiting.

GHISLAIN: Falsehood fools us with the evident, deforms reality. It replaces the sum-of-all-evidence reality by a fantastical reality. The equivalence "a policeman is a policeman, a gangster is a gangster" no longer holds. The evidence no longer indicates any reality. Falsehood rules.

COURRÈGE: Yes, so, what next?

GHISLAIN: All liars are fantasizers. So anyone who insists on understanding reality as a sum of all evidence will be fooled. So, then...

COURRÈGE: Yes, go on...

GHISLAIN: So fantasy envisioned as reality blurs the set of evidence that suspends the principle of non-contradiction. Essentially, falsehood is reality under the regime of fantasy, which makes reality and this other evidence agree—evidence that masks the blurred or ridiculed evidence, like the principle of non-contradiction.

COURRÈGE: What you're ultimately saying is that falsehood conceals the evident by transforming reality into fantasized evidence.

GHISLAIN: Falsehood exists because we fantasize. Otherwise, we wouldn't be duped.

COURRÈGE: Explain.

GHISLAIN: The idea is very simple, actually. The more we distort the evidence of reality by projecting our fantasies onto it, the more we'll be subject to falsehoods. The more we lie to ourselves, the more we'll be fooled by others' lies.

COURRÈGE: And if we take Scorsese's film as an example, how would you apply what you've just explained to it?

GHISLAIN: Well... give me a minute...

COURRÈGE: Okay.

She takes a bite of her sandwich.

Ghislain takes a bite of his sandwich.

COURRÈGE: You can think it over and write me.

GHISLAIN: I have two or three ideas.

COURRÈGE: Go on.

GHISLAIN: For example, Captain Queenan dies because he didn't consider the danger that the gangster-mole posed to his police department. Almost inexplicably, this cautious and informed man suddenly becomes naive and forgets that he could be followed. The fantasy of invincibility and the evidence of routine (even though a detective should never succumb to routine) are what blind the captain. Captain Queenan experiences the consequences of falsehood himself.

COURRÈGE: Yes, and are there other examples?

GHISLAIN: The entire film is built on this principle. In fact, every murder happens in response to a falsehood. This is what we must take away from the story. There is no murder without falsehood. Whether this is a passive lie (evidence that the person who is being pursued misses and which helps their capture, and which is supported by the fantasy of instinct, the idea that instinct is a good guide) or an active lie (some of the evidence has been deliberately hidden, therefore transforming reality into a series of fantastical evidence).

COURRÈGE: Every murder covers up a lie.

GHISLAIN: I would even say, despite what Laurent-Michel Vacher (whom I like very much) might think, that there is no death without falsehood.

* * *

I open and close my front door.

All I remember, all that comes back to me, are the moments just before this conversation and the moments just after it.

6. THE GUYAUDIAN

Courrège was sitting across from me, chewing her shawarma in one of the many internationally-themed food courts that exist in the underground tunnels of Montreal, between the Thai, Japanese, Mexican, Lebanese, Greek, Chinese, and Vietnamese food counters. My shish taouk had dripped on my paper plate, my chair wobbled, the surrounding decor had the pervasive kitsch and glitter of the future.

Our eyes locked.

The stunning gaze of friendship does not resemble that of love. A distinct, fragile, luminous gaze settled on my person. I'm not in love. No. But the seduction worked all the same. I thought it right to return her gaze, dive into her eyes, all the while controlling myself like someone who knows their proper place.

At first, I held her gaze as a challenge. And then for a few seconds more. But how long can we tolerate staring at the other person, face to face, without awakening something?

The thought came to me, the thought dissolved, the thought re-assembled, the thought reappeared. Suddenly, I had an overwhelming desire to fuck Courrège, to grab her passive, tender, listening body. A few seconds of sustained looking. That's all it took. Ninety-five thousand neural connections later, and a world of biochemical impulses fired up, I was there. Courrège, my old friend, a girl with no fiery sexual aura, a sweet, young woman, an intellectual, somewhat funny, protected by the walls of straight pants and the ramparts of gentleness, too selfless to be real.

* * *

I've never liked Basile's poems. At their best, they were lesser Denis Vaniers (his *Iconostase pour Pier Paolo Pasolini**); at their worst, they were amateurish sketches, a bit pompous or mediocre (his *Journal poétique*[†]). For me, Basile was a novelist and a critic, first and foremost. For others, he had been an agent of counterculture, the founding member of the magazine *Mainmise*[‡] (drug culture, underground movements, gay literature, feminism, etc.). Furthermore, the third volume of his Montreal trilogy, the French edition of which was published by Grasset (just like the first two volumes), had been titled *L'acide*. In Quebec, we'd contented ourselves with a different exotic title, *Les Voyages d'Irkoutsk*[§], much less provocative. However, I had looked through his work enough to find something that corresponded to my latest whims.

The Indebted Recluse
by JEAN BASILE

Hermit in your earthly cell
you pay dearly
for your solitude

---

* *Iconostase pour Pier Paolo Pasolini: Discours poétique sur les gays, le féminisme et les nouveaux mâles* [Iconostasis for Pier Paolo Pasolini: A Poetic Discourse on Gays, Feminism and the New Male], published in 1983. (Trans.)
[†] *Journal poétique, 1964–1965: Élégie pour apprendre à vivre, suivie de pièces brèves* [Poetic Journal, 1964–1965: Elegy for Learning to Live, Followed by Some Short Works], published in 1965. (Trans.)
[‡] *Takeover*. (Trans.)
[§] The French edition of Basile's novel was called *Acid*, while the Quebec edition was called *The Travels of Irkoutsk*. (Trans.)

That's why
when this pure state
becomes illusory
and you know it
you hold it against
everyone and yourself

(From his *Journal poétique*)

For me the recluse represented an archaic model of humanity who stood for the status quo, cessation and withdrawal, corrective mortification.

Is there a morality independent of obligation or sanction that can allow life to blossom and revere our actions rather than our fears? A scientific, atheist, natural morality that supports human cohabitation while also valorizing individualism?

In any event, fantasizing about Courrège, naked and available, I was at the mercy of my sudden urges. There I was, half-guilty of imagining a pornographic sex scene with my oldest friend when all I had to do was invite her over and kiss her.

Somewhere in the world was a book that was going to sustain me.

A morality independent of obligation or sanction.

An agnostic and natural morality.

The idea was clear and necessary. No doubt, the book had been written.

I told myself that I couldn't begin to persuade Courrège to have sex, I couldn't try to convince her without literary arguments. After all, I am Ghislain the reader and I live in the readopolis. I have to account for my actions and deeds to the

World Confederation of Books (WCB), to the Infinite Library of Completed and To-Be-Completed Books (ILCCB). If the desired book doesn't exist, it means that I haven't searched for it enough or that it's still too soon. Or that I should write it. [In fact, I had made bets, especially with Courrège and a few times with Maldonne, on certain predictions: I predicted when certain books on specific subjects would be published. Predicting new biographies of famous people was too easy to be interesting. All three of us predicted a biography of the boxer-poet Stéphane Ouellet one year before anyone else. Once you get to that point, it's no longer a game.

It was more interesting to foresee the types of stories or forms, characters or ideas that would come up in books over the more or less long term—but not less than one year in advance. Otherwise, it wouldn't be challenging. The more complex and precise our predictions were, the more points we won. We needed to predict, for example, when a European or American trend would reach Quebec, when a particularly racy subject would find a talented author capable of handling it well, when a young talent would squash a dominant literary figure and with what kind of novel (since the world of letters only has room for one or two dominant figures. Beyond this number, it all falls into exuberant anonymity. The media space, the public mental space can tolerate only a tiny number of literary players.)

The three of us—Courrège, Maldonne and I—all subscribed to an Anglophone website for predicting the destinies of books, *The Official Wizard of Books* (run by a fanatic from Chicago). Via the Anglophones, we had also found *Penguins and Porcupine* (the website of a Franco-Ontarian that referred to two major English publishing houses) and *Le devin des livres* (a badly designed site run by a partying Frenchman who was trying to copy *Wizard of Books*). I, too, intended to create our own site of literary predictions. I wanted to call it *L'Oracle des ombres* in honour of Michel Beaulieu.* But the time had not yet come. We already had fun in our approximate English, and our respective blogs, especially Maldonne's and her MySpace, kept us fairly busy.]

Here we are. It was easy, I found it by cross-referencing two or three things. A mere few seconds. I found a name: Jean-Marie Guyau. The book, in its 1898 translation by Gertrude Kapteyn, is called *A Sketch of Morality Independent of Obligation or Sanction*, and was first published in 1885, in Paris, as *Esquisse d'une morale sans obligation ni sanction*.

It was too perfect.

I quickly got on the BAnQ's website > Iris Catalogue. Ten seconds.

Fayard reprinted this book in 1985, as part of its "Philosophy Books in the French Language" series. (Note to English readers: the book has been reprinted by Forgotten Books.)

I didn't bother placing the copy on hold.

* * *

I thought of Maldonne. At times, I succumbed to self-criticism. At times, I passionately deconstructed myself.

With Courrège, it was Courrège. With Maldonne, it was more complicated. Our ambiguous understanding plagued me. Sure, I had felt a—let's call it secondary—attraction for

---

* Beaulieu published a poetry collection called *Oracle des ombres* [Oracle of Shadows] in 1979. (Trans.)

Courrège, but was it real? What did true desire look like—this thing made so commonplace in tons of books? Yes—Guyau. Yes, my interest in the ethics of anomie, the natural morality of the common stream of mortals. Yes—Maldonne as well. The stimulus and the cold mouth (to be filled with a complicit breath), my penis erect like a lead soldier. Courrège isn't the one I want to fuck, it's Maldonne through Courrège. Even for me, it's byzantine.

Metro Préfontaine, the subway station of a former mayor. Escalator, concrete. The grey walls, the strident colours of painted metal, the tunnels of sallow calcium, the *Métro* newspaper stands all passing by. A huge, red-orange Maccano structure that lets rain, wind, and dirt filter in.

I slide my pass, *shlonk!*

I notice a guy shuffling around, wedged into a coat with grotesque pockets and overalls the colour of a children's TV show, handing out leaflets to people getting off the train. Looking naive with his pack of 8.5" x 11" sheets, he seems almost happy to be distributing his tracts.

He walks towards me.

I greet him. He hands me a leaflet. He tells me that first, we are plants, then we become human. He explains it all in two treatises that he's willing to give me for free, though I insist on paying him. Two dollars, which he quickly pockets, thanking me. I stare at the pocket over his left knee; it's patched-up with colourful felt fabric. He's like a character from *Sesame Street* let loose on the streets of Montreal.

My example begins towards the end of my life as a plant, when I was about twenty-five years old.

He has written an allegorical text with cheerful flair, an adaptation of his socio-spiritual life, by resorting to the metaphor of metempsychosis. First, he was a plant: *The walls of his apartment were bark.* Then he ventured out on the street and became an insect, moved from one stage to the next in the chain of being: *Not quite knowing in what direction he should lead his life, he became a silverfish.*

In the next treatise, he describes his life on the streets, this time using the language of role-playing games, like *Dungeons and Dragons,* and *The Lord of the Rings,* the ultimate fantasy novel. *Clerics and priests are those who collect. Many people stop to tell them about their lives or their problems. The good priests will listen to them. Other passersby sometimes give them money to indirectly make amends for a past mistake (a question of karma, I imagine).*

But then came the orcas: *Orcas drink a lot of beer and have no manners. They look like punks, with their piercings and tattoos. Many people are afraid of them.*

Lastly came the vampires: *You cannot become a vampire without the help of another vampire. The same goes for drug dealers, they need a dealer higher up than them.*

Thousands of photocopyist writers wander America's streets, distributing their fleeting wisdom, their conclusions on life. I had met one of them. I had met the last herald of our modern cities, the son of Hermes and the Gorgon, a creature who freezes our blood with a gaze full of hope, while giving us a smile. On paper, he circulated reassuring maxims about a distressing world. A discreet ferryman of words with no intermediary, of emancipated hardship, he was an ally of *Megaphone* magazine, a brother who acted alone, a bearer of the merits of difficult self-accomplishment. A being who had come straight out between the legs of liberty, if not born from the unlikely union of urban mythological figures.

Was I a vampire or an orca? Had I gone beyond the insect stage. Had I donned wings?

I needed to see things clearly.

(In my non-relation with Maldonne, in my literary proselytizing, in my reading of Guyau.)

BenGharok@yahoo.com ended his treatise with this sentence:

In time, you will cross the bridge connecting the world of logic to the world of imagination and be able to see yourself clearly!

* * *

I was in a pre-emptive state. I felt a strong desire to buy two specific things before anyone else did.

Pre-emptive. From pre-emption, the action of purchasing before others.

It's as though the dictionary is trying to hold running water in its bare hands.

I felt the feverishness of acquisition. My feet led me to the Couche-Tard at the Joliette stop. This wasn't about work, but frenzy. A mania pushing me to procure, before anyone else, Saturday's *Le Devoir* and a bag of blue shark gummies.

Why did I have this frantic craving for inessential things: a Saturday newspaper and a bag of blue candy in the shape of sharks. Bad question (no answer in sight).

I thought of Guyau, of his formidable idea of *moral fecundity*. A thinker tugging at the conventions of thought. He introduces a pitch and sets the tone. He is a musician against complacency.

His thesis was simple and compelling: "He who does not act as he thinks, thinks incompletely." Also: "It may be said that will is but a superior degree of intelligence, and that action is but a superior degree of will. From that moment, morality is nothing else than *unity* of being. Immorality, on the contrary, is a dividing into two—an opposition of different faculties, which limit each other." This track of pre-emptive acquisition led me back to Guyau. This "need" was someone else thinking in my place, therefore colonizing my moral territory. A loss of unity. I was not thinking completely. Someone was thinking for me, someone had invaded my ethical autonomy. Furthermore, I was actually thinking this need. So I had to fulfil it, otherwise I wouldn't be able to think completely. Herein lay the whole problem of contemporary western life. All excess is good; all that is good is excess. The powerful image of the blue sharks and the *Devoir*, and experiencing the same rush of salivation for the gummies as for the *Devoir*'s literary pages, definitely made me think of Pavlov's experiments.

I read Guyau to convince myself of the contrary, and in a way, he applied himself to thwarting my desire to be convinced. I don't know if you follow. At this point I must admit, I am myself grasping at straws.

Guyau's ethics of anomie was the organic solution to morbid nostalgia, to our thousand opinions on euthanasia, abortion, the death penalty, the right to make mistakes, the influence of culpability and confusion.

No sanction. No obligation.

Moral fecundity as libertarian and responsible sovereignty.

I was surprised to find the fitting terms to reflect this ethics of anomie in the intuitive vocabulary of hockey players. *We were under pressure.* What is this pressure? *To be under pressure.* Guyau gives this cliché the full weight of a moral expression of anomie, the profundity of duty independent of obligation. He writes:

> There will always be found a kind of inner pressure exercised by the activity itself in these directions; the moral agent will, by a both natural and rational inclination, feel itself driven in that sense, and it will recognize that it has to make a kind of inner *coup d'état* to escape that pressure. It is this *coup d'état* which we call fault, or crime. In committing it, the individual does wrong to himself: he decreases and voluntarily extinguishes something of his physical or mental life.

The hockey player as the professor of contemporary moral philosophy. Why not? These are people who must constantly surpass themselves in a pagan context. The obvious paragon of a territory intended for the natural expression of an ethics of anomie.

Emergency over.

I will wait.

I sink back into Gombrowicz's *Ferdydurke*.

I've lost my craving for the blue sharks.

* * *

To: readmeagain@sympatico.ca
From: earnestoearnesto@gmail.com

Dear cinephile and moral exegete,

I miss you. Our movie night has transformed me into a curious talk show hostess resigned to listen to her guest of the week. It was unusual and delicious all at once. I'm not trying to come on to you. But I'm not trying to get out of it, either. Ah, we two love ambiguity, don't we! Never a dull moment...

There's only one copy of Guyau at the BAnQ. You're monopolizing it... So I haven't been able to look through it to answer you... to examine moral fecundity like you...

Your idea of moral fecundity reminds me of a kind of feminine pagan generosity. You know, a return to the mother goddess, to the primitive shelter of a generalized goodness that only needs to account for the survival of a human society based on a paradoxical matriarchy. An option that would no doubt give you shivers, like many other guyo...

I'm not insinuating that you're anti-matriarchy, I'm only posing the question. It seems to me that a morality without values, yet one structured around the concept of fecundity, expresses everything that still counts in this world that's stripped of everything and paradoxically filled from everywhere... When all that remains is life as an end in itself, yet unsurpassable and inalienable, fecundity becomes a magical phenomenon that subsumes all other epiphenomena still lagging behind old values plagued by various ideologies, dying beliefs and vague customs.

I am fecund, Ghislain, as much as any other woman. Don't let this realization terrify you! Anyway, shouldn't (moral) fecundity lead to peace?

The sound of peace is the sound of copulation, the sound of

the last cry before orgasm; it's the sound of a peaceful village before a summer storm; the sound of lipstick slowly sliding and spreading on the rosy and slightly moist lips of a woman who's about to give herself. The sound of peace is not silence, but the light tapping on a keyboard when we're writing to someone. The sound of peace is the sound of resilience, the sound of a human being joyously spitting out the seeds of fruit. The sound of peace is the internal sound, the sharp beating of organic valves suddenly recognizing a source of fecundity in the landscape, a reproductive source.

You know what I'd like? I have an idea. It's totally stupid, but sometimes I get these ideas (the sound of peace is also the sound of routine)...

Listen, can I come see you at the Couche-Tard? We could continue our conversation... The worst that could happen is that I'll transform back into a hostess and interview you... It wouldn't bother me... What do you think? I know that it's unusual, but then what isn't between us?

I'll wait to hear from you!

Take care!

Courrège
xxx

* * *

Friendliness is a slippery slope.

Courrège confronted me with her friendliness. For me, this was a challenge.

Yet the proximity of a friendly face is essential to our survival. If necessary, we can invent this face and superimpose it on those we meet, but the effect is not the same.

I was not in love with Courrège, and I couldn't explain it.

She was getting used to it. I was getting used to it.

It was as though I was running under a tiny, cartoonish cloud raining down on me. Cold water soaked my body.

Courrège was playing the little cloud, and I wasn't fighting it. It was dangerous.

I called her and invited her to drop by the next day, during my shift.

* * *

Stunning nature has spoiled us with the luxury of power, of potential.

Actually, I want to take up Guyau's writing once again. We live with texts inside us as though they were monkeys climbing and clinging onto our consciousness, despite fatigue and repeat warnings.

Writing is a learned animal that shakes us.

I lost Guyau. He escaped from my pores, like a liquid with a strange volatility. I felt the regular movement of secretions stirring my body, sometimes with blinding fierceness. A nourishment that had sustained me during a mental exercise, Guyau's book was producing its waste water, its fluids of intellectual anti-prostration.

We think "yes, yes, moral fecundity, of course," then we keep reading, we assimilate, we chew then digest the thought, then we think "here is an important author who tried to define an ethics of anomie without laws, a kind of methodical anarchist," then we start to doubt, to recognize rhetorical holes in the text, arguments that are somewhat slack and collapse in the face of our natural scepticism.

Then we arrive at this conclusion: "Isn't it in fact a work about power, an examination of natural morality regulated by our animal potential?" It would be too perfect if we were right. It would be too simple, of course. We circle around the subject. We are living beings who can. We are living beings who will continue being able in a society that regiments potential. We are living organisms who know they are alive, who recognize their freedom relative to the social overseer.

Returning to the book, I get the unbelievable urge to type once and for all a quote that's as revealing as it is deliciously empty: "As we have already explained, instead of saying, *I must, therefore I can*, it is more true to say, *I can, therefore I must*. Hence a certain *impersonal duty is created by the very power to act*. Such is the first natural equivalent of the mystical and transcendental duty."

If a resolute agnostic tells us we can, that's fine. But if he tells us that, because we can, we'll be faced with many natural duties, responsibilities inherent to humanity's natural power to act, what immediately comes to mind?

And is what comes to mind good?

I'm ashamed, I'm embarrassed. Four-colour display stands. Forsaken books on a hideous cardboard stand with eye-catch-ing design. He's the one I want to talk about, the conqueror: *the businessman.*

Why do businessmen take themselves for "philosophers"?

In what country are we living?

It's no doubt monstrous to associate a philosopher like Guyau with a businessman like Edmond Bourque, but how can one avoid relating them? They both teach the non-ideological ideology of potential that rules everything, that contributes to both success and social problems.

Edmond Bourque, *Choosing to Succeed – A Practical Guide in 9 Steps and 36 Easy Keys* (Forward by Alain Bouchard), Les éditions QualiPerformance.

What was the man's title? President and CEO of Couche-Tard? Professor at the HEC Montréal business school?

I'm not sure anymore. We sold his book. He was next to the coffee machine. He ruled from his cardboard display stand, sharing his recipe for success with the coffee drinkers that happened to come by.

Pinocchio's amusement park comes to mind.

A Couche-Tard with amusement rides, in which all the children slowly transform into donkeys, servile beasts imprisoned by their desire for indolence, for unreserved entertainment.

A park of perverted potential.

Mental health is the prerogative of true thinkers, and I was only a reader, doubling as a consumer of potato chips, chocolate bars, cheese sticks, and packaged popcorn, beer, coffee, and all kinds of newspapers. I was contributing to the smooth functioning of the carnival of poverty, desire, common interests that make the wheels of economy turn, paying truckloads of riches to the rich, and with increasing difficulty, hospital care for the poorest of the poor. Was Bourque ultimately my true master, the one who regulated my potential without my being aware of it?

* * *

It's the evening when Courrège will be dropping by.
To prepare myself, I thought that printing out a small batch of Super 7 results would make my work easier.
Plenty of change in the till.
The coffee machine is full.
My potential is at maximum.
It's fine. I become a Couche-Tard cashier once again.
I'm alive. That's what counts.

* * *

The human race publishes a book every thirty seconds.
—GABRIEL ZAÏD

I don't amuse myself by speaking; I live by speaking but I amuse myself by reading. I wouldn't know how to live without these small linguistic packets that everyone collects in their own way, sticks back together like old pieces of an endless puzzle, always metamorphosing.

If in Gutenberg's time, in 1450, 100 books were published annually for a population of 500 million inhabitants and, in 2000, one million books were published annually for a population of six billion inhabitants, it would be reasonable to predict than in 100 years, when more than twelve billion people will populate the earth, we will feed readers around the world over two million books annually, that is, one book every fifteen seconds.

A 6/49, a pack of Belvedere, a copy of *La Presse*.

From behind my counter, elevated by what the manager calls "the podium," I'm thinking.

A pack of citrus-flavoured Chiclets gum.

What stuns me in this procession of books that secretly terrify us is the fact that a published book calls forth another, that the organic structure of publishing naturally functions according to an exponential model.

A new author is born, two reviewers are born. A new scientific field emerges, three popularizing writers will be called to the task. Every published author awakens a writing vocation in two or three members of her extended family. Every famous author drags in his wake a handful of epigones, admirers who will become authors themselves one day.

A bag of cheese curds, a 500 ml bottle of Tropicana juice.

Courrège is late.

She's picking up Maldonne's habits.

A box of S.O.S. A litre of Montclair water.

Hawkers of the obvious also find their audience. Edmond Bourque is proof of this.

The continuum of satisfaction goes on. Someone is always in the dep. As soon as I have a moment alone, I sneak up to the coffee machine and return with a copy of Bourque's book. To propose a social activity to Courrège.

(Otherwise, for a total parody of these pop psychology books that readily crop up like morel mushrooms in a field of conifers devastated by fire, I recommend an elegant book by François Blais, *Iphigénie en Haute-Ville*,* published by L'instant même.)

COURRÈGE: I'm not too late?!

She wasn't too late. It was okay.

As soon as the latest customer leaves with his *Journal de Montréal*, I propose my game to her. I'll give her a page number and she'll read a paragraph of Bourque's book to me.

GHISLAIN: Listen, let's play a game.

COURRÈGE: You don't want me to help you a bit?

GHISLAIN: No need.

COURRÈGE: You sure?

GHISLAIN: Yes, yes.

COURRÈGE: But you're on camera!

GHISLAIN: They tape me to see if I filch a pack of gum or forget to card a minor.

COURRÈGE: Okay, have it your way.

GHISLAIN: I'm a spy. A double agent like Aquin. I gather information about the vast world in order to understand it better. I'm only trying to discover what mosquito bit us.

COURRÈGE: But what do you get out of always being in a precarious position like that?

GHISLAIN: I'm not in a precarious position. I analyze, I read.

COURRÈGE: And then?

GHISLAIN: I read, *ergo* I think, *ergo* I am. Of necessity, I take up more space than others, I assume more space in the great symbolic machine.

GHISLAIN (*to customer*): Yes, sir. You want the Super 7 re-

---

* *Iphigenia in Upper Town*. (Trans.)

sults? Here you go. An Export "A" King Size Extra Light. Here you go. Thank you. Until next time!

COURRÈGE: Do you realize just how much of a hypocrite you can be?

GHISLAIN: Have you seen the two *Clerks* movies by Kevin Smith?

COURRÈGE: Yes.

GHISLAIN: There's your answer.

COURRÈGE: What answer? That vulgarity and frustration rule the world? That stupidity and all types of inferiority complexes are existential stimulants? I write to you because I consider you to be a special human being, not a fart bag for retarded adolescents!

GHISLAIN: You're really sexy when you're angry.

COURRÈGE: Stop talking nonsense.

GHISLAIN: I swear.

GHISLAIN: $3.67 ma'am. Thank you! Please come see us again!

GHISLAIN (*handing Bourque's book to Courrège*): Go to page 61. Read me some of that nonsense.

COURRÈGE (*flipping the pages*): "We can often observe a difference of opinion between individuals who live or work together, tacitly expressed by a facial reaction in conversation, by a shift in tone in the language or writing style."

GHISLAIN: A coffee, a *Journal de Montréal*, a ham sandwich, $6.80. Thank you! Until next time!

GHISLAIN (*to Courrège*): Bourque bombards us with the evident. The obvious.

COURRÈGE: I think it's well-written.

GHISLAIN: Yes, well, beyond the clear formulation, you agree with me that everything he says is obvious.

COURRÈGE: It's his fifth key. He calls it "the necessity of collaboration."

GHISLAIN: He has thirty-six just like it. Would you want to buy this pack of banalities?

COURRÈGE: I don't know. Everyone seeks guidance. I imagine that the owner of Couche-Tard wanted to circulate his mentor's ideas.

GHISLAIN: $8.92, sir! Thank you! Please come see us again!

GHISLAIN: You don't find that sad?

COURRÈGE: What should I find sad?

GHISLAIN: You don't find the *racket* of the obvious sad? As though no one had ever learned anything, as though no one had the least bit of initiative? You don't find it sad that an adult feels the need to be told that he should learn to collaborate in order to get on in life?

COURRÈGE: It's not a bad thing to be reminded of the obvious.

GHISLAIN: But the obvious is what friends are for; it's what conversation is for! Family, loved ones, friends, girlfriends, boyfriends should be the ones dealing with the obvious, not a book!

COURRÈGE: I don't see why not a book.

GHISLAIN: The Bible also states the obvious, but at least it's coated in a good stew of ambiguities, horrors, tales, incomprehensible things, and poems. It's much closer to life, ultimately. It deserves to be read because it's complex, at times as dense as a Basile novel.

COURRÈGE: Why do you think so many cooking shows exist?

GHISLAIN: Cooking... Everybody loves to eat, don't they?

COURRÈGE: Because people are fascinated by successful recipes. Because people love to be given advice, because they're lazy. Because they like to watch Josée di Stasio chatting while cutting onions.

GHISLAIN: Reading Bourque is like cutting onions or reading a successful recipe?

COURRÈGE: Absolutely. Just like diets, the recipe for success is always miraculous, even if what it conveys is obvious. People still want to read the story of Mister "if you want it, you can do it." They're still interested in the experience of a "I did all the steps took my time persevered stayed patient and I succeeded," as well as the difficulties of Madam "I overcame a great challenge fought against prejudice met my soul mate" or even Mister or Madam "I sacrificed my life for the children's happiness I neglected all my talents for a good cause."

GHISLAIN: A *Lundi*, a *Journal de Montréal*, a large bag of Lay's Old Fashioned Bar-B-Q chips. $9.96. Thank you, ma'am! Until next time!

COURRÈGE: I'm not against cheap hope.

GHISLAIN: If hope means having a bit of future pleasure, I could say that I sell instant hope, here at Couche-Tard.

COURRÈGE: You sell instant satisfaction to those in need of it.

GHISLAIN: It's pretty sad. My job is sad.

COURRÈGE: You're the one who's sad, Ghislain.

* * *

In my bed, late at night.

I started thinking about the scene when Harry and Adletsky meet in Saul Bellow's novel, which I had just been reading (*The Actual*, Viking, 1997). A famous billionaire invites a known writer to come see him. An unexpected appointment. Harry, with the main narrator's voice in tow, shows up. The conversation begins. Each deserves the other's esteem. No faux pas. No one loses, each wins in this comical struggle to impress the other. Soon Harry and Adletsky find their point in common: they both understood the purpose of a grand society dinner. Behind the smokescreen of gowns and wandering hands, a woman and a man had a score to settle. The climax of the show, the nodal point uniting the network of guests, had escaped everyone except the writer and the billionaire.

Adletsky tells him: "Anyway, I thought I'd like to become acquainted with somebody like you—a first-class noticer obviously."

A writer = a first-class noticer.

I fell asleep turning this thought over in my mind: all first-class noticers open the door to a universe that goes beyond themselves.

My life is twisted up, dying in an ashtray that's no longer smouldering. An old panicky film, blurry scenes, cracks in narrated platitudes are not enough to allow me a respite. I dream that I'm not dreaming. More than a summons, it concerns a gradual, horizontal precipice. A highway lined with old dwarf palms bloating up plaster pots. Silence. I don't hear anything. A long shot that will become the narrative blurs what I'll do to Courrège.

I walk down the hallway. I see Saul Bellow's door. He's there, a great among greats, slumped over by the door. His face lies in a puddle of Cuban rum. I pull on his arm. He stands up on his own, impassive and dignified. I open the door. A young

Bellow greets me. His mischievous head is buried in the folds of the soft leather couch. He throws a cotton ball at me. I sit up. I have fallen under his desk, I'm scratching his legs. I'm bent on trying to hide, to flee an obligation I can't recall. I'm forced to perform a task that gnaws at me. I sweat. Laugh. Bite. Think. Speak. At the same time, I'm worried. I emit groans that make sense. Then my conversation improves. The young Bellow seems to be listening to me. I feel camaraderie grow between us. We go back into the hallway. There's a puddle of Cuban rum on the floor. No one notices it.

I have a bunch of keys.

I know that one of them will open the most important door in the hallway.

I concentrate.

The young Bellow runs in a zigzag, kicking everything. But I'm fixed to the spot, frozen in a solemn pose. I leave behind a concentrational space. I dissolve into the evident. I slip into a Prague of silent film, a Prague of Orson Welles filming *The Trial*.

I carry on a long process of depersonalization.

I'm pulverized into read books. I'm dispersed among dreamt books, books watched onscreen, filmed books.

Inflated with moral air, I slowly empty and land on a patched-up sofa in the office of the child Bellow.

He eyes me from head to toe, suspicious—an expression that's totally new to him. I'm unmasked.

I stretch.

I slide the button on the clock radio.

Gypsy music invades my bedroom.

Pause.

7.

NEXT EPISODE, CHICAGO: THE OFFICIAL WIZARD OF BOOKS

PAUSE.
Something that stops time, suspends it.

John-Esther Greengrass has just left his mental universe to reappear among the natural chaos of beings. He is walking alone on a street in Chicago's Loop. He's carrying his *dernier cri* eReader.

Tired of his own company, the way we get tired of keeping death company or visiting family, Greengrass has little tolerance for a lack of social density. It's summertime in Chicago, and no one notices summer when the sun is shining. Greengrass doesn't notice it. He is wandering around without thinking. He is wandering around convinced that wandering involves nothing better than alleviation. He is wandering around with the carefree attitude of people who know nothing better than themselves, in a world where the Great Self sums up life.

He's a fine man, tall and handsome, elegantly muscular. A neutral haircut, dyed when needed. Energetic and impatient, charming in society, he quickly irritates those he makes more or less affectionate targets. He doesn't accept the natural mediocrity of things and beings. In general, nothing aligns with his very classy vision of life. He only reveres stereotypes. In a comic book, he would have played the role of the melancholic womanizer, a sort of chic geek. Actually, Greengrass is an architect. He has money and spends it on prostitutes. All in all, he is an excellent specimen of the era.

Greengrass likes his city and everything in it that relates to the water, to its flow. Chicago is a city of water, a strange Venice of the Great Lakes.

He has developed a theory about interpersonal relationships, a kind of barometer for measuring interactions with others. He tells whoever will listen that every human being functions according to a different relational programming code, that each of us has asymmetrical relational abilities and that, to survive decently in society, we need to learn to understand and anticipate each person's level of relational tolerance. From fifteen seconds to a whole lifetime, the spectrum is vast! But it is possible, according to his theory, to get along with anyone if we can discover the ideal length of interaction with that individual.

Still walking at a fast pace, he watches a video clip on his cell phone. Thirty seconds of a magnificent Moroccan woman belly dancing in his apartment. Too much of a turn-on to look away. A night's experience duly archived.

His good friend (but what could this mean in his case?) Hubert Lucrecios, a bookseller at Barnes & Noble, never tires of seeing this refined young woman with pointed breasts and the fertile hips of a professional.

Greengrass feels some pride in this sudden infatuation.

* * *

In a huge bookstore, we can hide out and be forgotten.

Hubert Lucrecios is serving a woman who accompanies him to the esoteric books department. All these books answer or seem to answer essential, serious, sad questions. Who are we? Why do we suffer? Why is life so difficult? Why am I not important to others? Are we lizards or the children of extraterrestrials? What is the secret of life? Can an incurable disease be cured by will alone? Can stones protect us against negative spirits and bad energy? How many times will we be reincarnated? Can our previous souls teach us about what we will become? Can we communicate with our ancestors' ghosts? How many spirits are able to speak through me? Will I too discover the master key system? Can I change my life and become someone else by reading a book that promises so? Can I communicate with my plants and my dead daughter?

Lucrecios would gladly burn down these con jobs. Every time he brings customers to the esoteric section, he feels as though he's vaporizing their brains with an acidic and corrosive substance.

No one seems to glimpse even the barest minimum amount

of healthy hope in the uncertainty principle. When Lucrecios deigns to offer some pertinent advice, he recommends to the most alert of these book zombies that they read *The Wisdom of Insecurity* by Alan W. Watts. The author's harsh but clear statement, his intelligent way of getting people to consider uncertainty and insecurity as beneficial objects of thought rather than obstacles to meaning, aligns in every respect with the problems posed by today's godless reality, this ambiguous reality beset by the scientific uncertainty principle. What we know today will be obsolete tomorrow. The author of this book (which was published in 1951) urges us to relativize, to deal with reality within the limits of our knowledge without hoping to draw out much more.

Chicago, 2006. No one believes in anything anymore, except in Oprah Winfrey, architecture, and sex.

Religion is no longer established around a book and various commandments, but around lobby groups, when it's not working to create itself. Today, opinion conveniently replaces belief, and thus acts as scientific belief because it is quantifiable and falsifiable all at once (see Karl Popper's principle). Being religious today means checking the boxes on an electronic form; it means answering a computer voice in monosyllables and getting satisfaction from completing a task without understanding its importance and why we always feel a grotesque sense of serious purpose in accomplishing it.

Ultimately, it's difficult to sympathize without also feeling contempt for all these good people looking for an easy answer. One that resolutely draws a veil over the world.

Lucrecios quickly returns to his workstation to do another search. He blows his nose, then carefully crumples up the dirty tissue and throws it in the garbage can under the counter.

Embroidered in his duties like a glass bead in a large hooked rug, Greengrass's friend sometimes finds the time long and gets annoyed at the smallest thing, yet also keenly understands his role in this noble business dedicated to books. A bitter low-wage earner and an idealist convinced that he is anything but, Lucrecios doesn't really know how to envision his future, but he knows that today he will complete his bookseller tasks and punch out his card as an average employee, without the risk of lending his name to a street or park.

In the evening, he returns to his computer, his tender window. He has learned to forgive thanks to technology. At the moment, his outlet is *The Official Wizard of Books*, which keeps him extremely busy.

His meal finished, he spends time scribbling his bibliophilic reflections in the void.

On this website, Lucrecios predicts the titles of books to come, books that will be published in the near future, within a maximum of five years. For fans of bibliophilic sites, he has literally become the Nostradamus of the publishing world. As he has been working on this project for only three years, some of his literary prophesies have not yet come to pass. Some remain to be proven. But as soon as ten or twelve of his unusual predictions came true, his reputation flourished throughout the American literary web.

The following is a list of Lucrecios's predictions that came true, books whose subject or thesis he had identified, or, in some cases, the almost exact formulation of the title:

The Cell Phone Cure: A New Urban Ethics by Michael Von Bullow, published by McCormick Medicine

Predicted on October 11, 2004
Published on May 7, 2006

*

TV Series Come to the Rescue of the Seventh Art by Emily S. Watson, published by University of Toronto Press

Predicted on April 10, 2004
Published on October 8, 2005

*

Weather Wars, New Weapons of Climate by John Parranditi, published by Soft Fiction

Predicted on September 2, 2004
Published on July 9, 2006

*

A Baby Named "Oil" by Lily Applegate, published by Picador

Predicted on May 18, 2004
Published on February 7, 2006

*

The Foolish Life of Joaquin Phoenix by Chris Birmingham, published by Altar & Wickermann

Predicted on August 2, 2004
Published on March 4, 2006

*

The Cynical Despair of Chuck Palahniuk by Mick Adler, published by the University of Illinois Press

Predicted on September 6, 2004
Published on July 25, 2006

*

I Killed My Mother's Fifth Clone by Aristid de la Toussaint, published by Perennial

Predicted on July 23, 2004
Published on January 8, 2006

*

Everyone Is "Security" by Abigaël Larivée, published by Random House

Predicted on August 23, 2004
Published on March 2, 2006

*

A Vampire in Kabul by Richard C. Newman, published by Tabloid Horror Country

Predicted on May 6, 2003
Published on October 16, 2006

*

The End of Movie Theatres by Tristan Butterfly, published by New York University Press

Predicted on January 9, 2004
Published on October 3, 2006

*

Textbook of a Young Serial Killer by Catherine Corner Rose, published by Public Press

Predicted on May 8, 2004
Published on July 11, 2006

* * *

No insider information. No particular contact with up-and-coming authors. No vigil in front of publishing houses. No secret line. No trivial advertising. No sales of banners, ad space or pop-up shops. No advisors recruited in university back rooms. No friends in print media. No friends in electronic media.
  (No friends.)

Only a hundred subscribers. Only a hundred fanatics of bibliophilic predictions. Only aficionados of the printed page. Only comical cynics bitten by the contemporary bug of book madness. Only enlightened fans practising divinatory sociology.

Greengrass doesn't take this endeavour seriously, in so far as Lucrecios accepts the publication of titles that are similar yet not exact. What matters is that the agenda of the title announced, predicted, comes to pass.

* * *

Lucrecios lives near Washington Park and the University of Chicago. A property inherited from a very good grandmother.

He lives at the corner of East 54th and Blackstone. An affluent neighbourhood, university residences, a British campus atmosphere, everything to signify the old-fashioned presence of books, the bygone indolence of the upper class, of professors in boaters and ladies with parasols.

Chicago welcomed jazz with its majestic parks, its urban forests woven by Olmsted, its grandiloquent sculptures celebrating the city's development.

Lorado Taft's *Fountain of Time* stretches out its concrete procession in homage to the fanatical ideology of progress as first imagined. A long series of eras, key figures, men, and women march, melted into one another, all turned towards the future, carrying their dreams in tow, biting into the fluid reality of time.

Lucrecios reaches Cottage Grove Avenue, greets the parrots in the park, a small colony of *Myiopsitta monachus*, cackling and whistling on the power lines at the corner of East 54th Street. The remnant of a university anomaly or an aviary escape, the presence of monk parakeets in the middle of the city has created an attraction. Unlike the inhabitants of Cottage Grove and 54th Street, Lucrecios finds them picturesque and sees in them a sense of liberating and ironic psittacism.

He would gladly transform Greengrass into a parrot and fucking leave him on a perch in a pet shop window.

He would do the same with Christina Baldacci.

How to get rid of an ex without coming off as a psychopath? Ah, a good title.

He sits on a park bench to write it down. The world of ideas resembles a fountain of time, and Lucrecios stuffs himself with ideas.

He will post this new title online. His Montreal friends will likely approve of his latest finding.

After his walk, he adds the title to his list of predictions: *How to Get Rid of an Ex Without Coming off as a Psychopath?*

He sees no reason why someone wouldn't write this book within two years.

A conservative estimate. Amusing titles are always the easiest to predict.

But, for reasons of conscience, and because he doesn't want to be pretentious, he indicates in the appropriate box next to the prediction: *Within three years*, then the date.

The phone rings. It's Greengrass. He doesn't answer, closes his shutters, turns off his computer, and goes to sleep.

* * *

— *Fuck you, poodle ass!*

7. NEXT EPISODE, CHICAGO

Christina Baldacci is screaming at the top of her lungs, swaying on a wobbly chair, shaking her fists in the air, brutally twisting her neck. Green Mill, 4802 North Broadway, the Uptown Poetry Slam.

Nobody's here, when I was born, I knocked on the door, gave the postman my car keys and the stray bomb I hatch under my shirt like an extra breast.

The spoken word poet leaves the stage under the deranged screams of drunk young men and young women in the grips of total paradoxical delirium. Everything unfolds by the book, in a fanatical meltdown, the school of "clash." Baldacci is tired of the awkward clichés of spoken word poets, though she slams on a regular basis, always repeating her "Fuck you, poodle ass!" without an employee ever putting her in her place. It's a colossal carnival of urban myth delivered by the labourers of a vulgar and common idiom, without affectation, devoid of any aesthetic concerns. It all unfolds on the fringes of Samsonites and BlackBerries, in a jazz club determined to resist good taste.

Baldacci gets the audience wrong.

People rush to Marc Smith's poetry slams with the same fury as to Wrigley Field.

Baldacci gets the audience and her body wrong. She frowns at the back of the room, yelling "Fuck you, poodle ass!" over and over, as though launched inside a panicky torpedo. She constantly pulls up the sleeves of her black fleece.

She broke up with Lucrecios because everything bores her: excitement bores her, egotists bore her, the media bores her, the *Chicago Tribune* bores her, slams bore her, poetry bores her even more, bad books bore her, good books bore her just as much, good sex bores her, acrobatic sex and tenderness bore her, large boulevards bore her, reversals in the water flow bore her, indigenous people bore her, colonialism bores her, educational comic books bore her, professors bore her, young pickpockets bore her, ditto Bresson's *Pickpocket*, literature in general bores her, Salinger with his reclusiveness and renown bores her and not just a little, Chicago's history bores her, democracy bores her, totalitarianism bores her, others bore her, gingerbread cookies bore her, Native Americans bore her, cynical people bore her, people bored by cynical people bore her, like super-mystical people, the monsoon season in Southeast Asia bores her and the one in Southwest Asia as well, religions bore her, work and lack of work bore her, electric crankshafts bore her, the Statue of Liberty bores her, *The Simpsons* bores her, Ben Stiller bores her, Emily Dickinson bores her, Hillary Clinton bores her, the Republicans bore her, convention delegates bore her, the voiceless bore her, the homeless too, Chicago's parrots bore her, Chicago's aquarium bores her, Chicago bores her, eating bores her, laughing bores her, toothbrushes bore her, old professors except Ms. Bartleman bore her, her cousin bores her, her birthday bores her, seduction bores her, her beauty and her breasts bore her, menstrual cramps bore her, truth bores her, lies too, ministers bore her, lobbyists bore her, mountain climbers bore her, confident people bore her, pop machines bore her, her house bores her, her clothes bore her, her teeth bore her, and her stainless steel refrigerator bores her.

In other words, Christina Baldacci is really bored.

Christina Baldacci gets her body wrong.

Yet Christina Baldacci never gets her organs wrong.

Everything leaves her liver to descend through the small intestine. To each their life.

* * *

Greengrass doesn't lie; he copulates with his daydreams. Not the same thing. In his spare and clean apartment, he's playing with a rubber ball. The ball bounces off the grey-white wall, hits the floor softly, then lands back in his hand and makes him happy. He's waiting for a prostitute. If only everything were this simple. "Perhaps the most exasperating thing about 'me,' about nature and the universe, is that it will never 'stay put.'" Watts wrote this statement, which Lucrecios had already formulated using the words "room" and "drama" or "tragedy." Sharing in the restlessness of the world means sharing in its success, in the important trajectories that will reshape the future, dishearten as many generations of human beings as possible, debase the new millennium with the force of dominant ideology.

* * *

The Chicago Spire, an immense spiralling drill bit, a twisting skyscraper of 150 floors, 610 metres high, will be for Chicago what the Lighthouse of Alexandria would have been to the metropolis of ancient Egypt: a new symbolic flame. The twisting structure will evoke a smoke spiral coming from Native American campfires along Lake Michigan, the first indigenous village established on its shores.

Projected cost: USD$2.4 billion. Architect: Santiago Calatrava. A Spanish master who will make his mark in the permanent exhibition of skyscrapers in Chicago, the birthplace of the skyscraper as we know it today—industrial spearhead in the geographical centre of the current economic empire. In other words, he will get his chance to build Rome.

Greengrass works for the major architecture firm Perkins+Will, who received the commission to build this unusual structure, to buoy the construction of the twisting drill bit that will rest on immense caissons of reinforced concrete. Among hundreds of architects, he designed the building's fenestration. Construction is set to begin in 2007 and be completed sometime in 2009.

Greengrass's work for the Chicago Spire was that of a dedicated employee. The noble task of an accomplished underling. But the project that's closest to his heart—the one for which he has been given real creative latitude so that he can add his own curve to the catalogue of walls in the world, a unique perspective that will make his name renowned, the project that motivates him and makes him smile, the one that consoles him in his dreary and repetitive life—is the Dykhouse project.

A house for an eccentric client that will cost over four million dollars. He finally has his hands on an inspiring contract.

So he is designing the fantasy house of an upstart. A businessman who made it big, who amassed a fortune by betting on the sales of granola bars. The Klondike and the granola bar.

Ball and bounce. Wall, wall and popliteal fossa, knee, arm, head.

There's a knock on the door.

The description matches. He puts away his ball.

* * *

Lucrecios is still asleep. He has trouble dealing with the remarks of the masses, the menus written in chalk in Chicago's pubs. He sleeps some more. Turns on his back. Sleeps some more. Takes his time yawning, rolling his body like a happy seal. Time soothes him. As though the captains of ghostly ships have decided not to bother him, not to wake him anymore. Lucrecios has no reason to dream. But he dreams. He imagines himself in the body of an imposing parrot, a parrot fit for a parade, insistent in gait, puerile in form.

Lucrecios flutters above Lake Michigan, soars over the old Polish neighbourhood, Washington Park, the skyscrapers of the Loop, and the beaches flanking the city.

He thinks he is Flaubert's parrot, the parrot of Félicité, a dedicated servant doomed to survive the cruelty of the world. Loulou is amusing, sneaks into people's houses, pokes them with his beak, catches them with their notorious gullibility and unenlightened faces.

Loulou doesn't condemn relevance, he gives it an enema.

Loulou doesn't tell a story, he collects touch phrases.

Loulou lives at the mayor's house, good old Harold Washington. The only biped in the area to gather good stories. A fragile hologram of a history of talent and birds.

Loulou and Lucrecios occupy the same body, work the same flying muscles, activate the same frontal lobe regions. Loulou-Lucrecios gorges on seeds offered by passersby. Nothing moves at the same speed as the day anymore. Everything slows down and accelerates according to unknown laws. A fictive pain and a fictive pleasure dwell in this zone.

Everything ends, of course, at Jimmy's Woodlawn Tap (on 55th Street). With a young Saul Bellow. Watching everyone like a hawk, while scribbling the phrases of a hypochondriac in a notebook.

* * *

I am not Herzog, I am a non walking sentimental philosopher who happens to dream about a millionaire...

* * *

No one today really remembers Christina Baldacci. They remember a look, a turn of phrase, her large breasts, her masculine jaw, but then what else? Not her name. Why? Because she never gives her real name. Besides, why should she give her real name?

When she sucks off a client; when she grips his balls in her mouth; when she reminds him that sex is only one drug among many; when she offers the flower of her asshole with unrivalled generosity (sometimes without a condom if they pay extra); when she decides to kiss an embarrassed client, a "baby" (she calls them "babies"), on the mouth, and he immediately falls in love; when she maternally hesitates before offering her ass to men electrified by embarrassment or excitement, she never gives her real name. For all these wretched men, she is Serena or Venus, depending on her mood.

* * *

Chicago burned to the ground in 1871. But its past remains intact. The Chicago River, the railroads, the commercial hub of America, the mercantile inventiveness (the invention of the department store, the mail-order catalogue and McDonald's), then a personality, Oprah Winfrey.

Somebody wants to hurt you
Somebody wants to get used by you
Somebody wants to abuse you
Somebody wants to be abused...

Christina Baldacci is getting ready to leave the Green Mill. She cautiously looks for some male prey.

Two passable guys in the middle of the room, but one has his head buried in his hands. No depressives or my-girlfriend-just-left-me tonight. Next.

A huge strapping man, elbows on the counter, is sipping a tall, colourful drink. He seems calm, stoical. He looks good. But perhaps the drink colour conceals certain perversions, certain sophisticated requests that she doesn't feel like satisfying. She wants a fuck with no strings, a roll in the sack with no complicated scenario.

A guy in his late forties walks over to a corner, greets a friend. They're not lovers. She doesn't look at him. He wants her, but she's looking for another "prospect." He's undoubtedly a bad lover, unable to arouse a minimum infatuation for the night.

Only the sound technician, a blasé waiter, and two guys laughing loudly near the stage remain.

The sound technician seems quiet, rolls his cables keeping his head down, walks with a nonchalant gait, lacks energy. Screwing on a special pocket spring mattress requires at least a minimum amount of energy.

The two laughing guys are an option. But their alliance

could be scary. *Those who laugh together go to war together.* She heard this Chinese saying in a university class. She's not afraid of anything, except others' laughter. Not their harmful laughter, their defensive laughter, their sadistic laughter, but their close-knit laughter, the laughter of a community defending the same prejudices. To choose, she would need to decide between them, separate them, sow seeds of discord. Too much effort.

Only the blasé waiter remains.

Pleasant physique. The pout of a stripper who doesn't have the courage to take his clothes off. Proud of his body. Slaving away, carrying trays of pints of beer. Steady arms. Hasn't spilled a drop. Unpretentious bearing. Doesn't shuffle around, but flies between the tables. Remains polite despite the traditional sarcastic remarks and two-penny jokes of the bar crowd. Pretends to be blasé, but it's her last card.

* * *

Lucrecios still can't believe it.

Without prior warning, the company's henchmen turned up at the bookstore in the middle of the day to fire his colleague Mat Clearwood, his companion in provisional liberty. The two get along famously, clearly admitting that they'll never make it out. It's a way of seeing things and of understanding the world. In any event, a form of caustic friendship sprang up between them.

Clearwood and Lucrecios see themselves as characters of the dusty and marginal crowd in Nelson Algren's books.

The truth is, Lucrecios is not at the level he would have

wanted to be at. Why doesn't he ever have the courage to show his anger? Why is he always afraid of taking up the whole room? Essentially, two things still salvage his dignity: his book-prediction website and his long solitary walks in the city.

Gas, masks, machines, robots, miniaturization, development, braggarts, dry lives, malfunctions, longshoremen confined to silence, proud ship of Argentinean officers on which people were tortured under the cover of beauty, smart walls, smartphones, smart appliances, wireless electricity, painless illness, continuous energy, weather monitoring, Asimov with his giant's beard laughing at having predicted everything, disposable hearts, regenerative skin, pageless books, uploaded knowledge (see *Fantastic Planet*, with Topor's drawings), telepathic crime, thought police.

And, on top of all this, now they fire his friend Clearwood? It's too much. Lucrecios has had enough.

He's going to write a letter to the *Chicago Tribune*. He's going to report this latest affront to liberty. He's going to sympathize with his ex-colleague.

Few people exist for the right reasons.

Few people manage to synchronize their ideas with their reason, their expectations with their passions, their vitality with their pride.

Few people risk some kind of sacrifice.

Don't say too much, don't go on forever. It's only a letter.

But the seriousness of the situation must be made obvious.

* * *

Wrongful Dismissal
at Barnes & Noble

Barnes & Noble has just casually dismissed one of its employees, a bookseller, on October 2, because he posted some unkind comments about the store's clientele (without naming them) on his Facebook wall.

Is this a precedent? How should we take this affront to freedom of expression?

It is an obvious fact that the majority of people don't like their jobs; they feel lost, underused, badly paid or demeaned. Work is a stopgap between financial necessity and integration in society. Many people manage to make the two ends meet by keeping a cool head and finding the appropriate professional tone and polite appearance. But underneath this social veneer, repressed recriminations, ordinary frustrations, and restrained anger most often lie hidden. All those who live to work and work to live have moments of doubt and spite, moments when they verbally lose control. Of course, when it comes to criticizing or complaining about our employers or our jobs, we're fortunate to have the safety valve of our friends and loved ones to absorb the shock. Who wouldn't be fired at least once in their lifetime if one day we would be able to read their thoughts? [...]

And so it continues, padded with opinionated naïveté and good intentions, all the way to the signature at the bottom.

* * *

Greengrass sits down first. He's made a reservation for two at La Petite Folie (on 55th Street). His treat.

GREENGRASS: A dismissal isn't death, right? Your friend messed up, lost his little job. Another little job is waiting for him... So what?

Lucrecios mumbles something to himself.

GREENGRASS: I have to tell you. A Cameroonian. I fucked a Cameroonian, really top-notch. I paid well, of course—why wouldn't I? A total babe, classy ass, shapely breasts, soft eyes. Like almond paste, all honey. Unabashed laugh, vulnerable smile. Totally right to not kiss me on the mouth at the end. Impeccable service. Pure. Know how much purity costs? Well, in Chicago, it costs about $140 an hour. Think about it.

LUCRECIOS: Listen... (*He's never managed to get interested in his friend's escapades with prostitutes.*)

GREENGRASS: You see, the effect of fucking lasts about two and a half hours. So when I leave the hotel room, it's like I remain attached to the girl's body for another hour and a half. It's the law of bewilderment.

Silence.

GREENGRASS: Every time we meet someone, we have a kind of time map inside us that starts to tick away seconds. Every time we meet someone, a small window pops up on our small onboard computer with a recommended time of interaction. Remember *Robocop*? The data that appears inside his helmet about the people he meets? We automatically assess how much time we should spend with an individual so that our bodies draw all the juice needed for intellectual and emotional metabolism. I'm sure of it. A Darwinist who gives lectures, spreading the good word of scientific atheism, talks about it, I think. What's his name, ugh, shit... I'm drawing a blank... He's on talk shows, gets thrown in the arena to put fear into Christian groups... You don't remember his name... Chris... or Gerard... or Michael... Studied at Oxford, I think. I saw an interview with him on TV just last month...

LUCRECIOS: Richard Dawkins. He wrote *The Selfish Gene*.

GREENGRASS: That's him!

LUCRECIOS: So your thing, it's a kind of empathy calculator?

GREENGRASS: No, not empathy, you don't understand what I'm trying to say. It's much simpler than that. It's not conscious. It's our body's way of marking out ports of time... Actually, we use a similar process when we learn how to read, for example, but in other parts of our brains... Now, look, about this dismissal business, Facebook is just today's way of filling up time for narcissists without families or affection, that's all. I don't want to get into racial profiling, but it's obvious, you know, they wouldn't dare fire you for such neurotic reasons because you're black. Imagine the scandal! A major bookstore chain, with its corporate image, culture, and books, firing a black man for stupid and superficial reasons!? Couple of calls to the media and it would all come out. We would relive the whole history of slavery, blacks, the Port of Dakar, Audubon, the Civil War, Martin Luther King, Malcolm X, Sidney Poitier, Miles Davis, Richard Wright, Edwidge Danticat, Jacques Stephen Alexis, Toussaint Louverture, Muhammad Ali, Will Smith, Colin Powell, Condoleezza Rice... You can't deny it... I'd even take to the streets with a sign to piss off my bosses, annoy my architect colleagues who bore each other stiff when they're not watching a Cubs or Blackhawks game or an independent film... You alone are an exclamation mark! Your friend's suffered a modern humiliation; you'd suffer an atavistic humiliation, a collective humiliation... You know, in a way, if you had taken it on, if Oprah would've decided to invite you to tell your story on the air, if people had taken the time to understand the kind of problem that will occupy the better part of our ideological debates in the near future, everything involving free speech and private life, maybe then we would've managed to speak frankly, once we'd dealt with the pathos, archival images, and TV tremors... Maybe we would've managed to speak seriously about the thought police, don't you think?

LUCRECIOS: Yeah, but I'm not the one they fired. As for the thought police, white people invented it. That's a fact. And it doesn't stop many blacks from being just as damn stupid as many whites. But it doesn't mean that we have to march when one of our friends—Asian, Mexican, black, white, Porto Rican or Native American—gets fired for a "thought crime"...

GREENGRASS: You don't understand anything about the bastards who govern us. Everything is public... We're living in the most public era of human history. It's obvious... And everyone likes it... Being known is no longer a privilege, it's a prerequisite for being part of society... Whoever isn't known around you doesn't exist in three dimensions. The new third dimension now is the fame of at least your name. I'm getting thirsty... Should we order a bottle?

* * *

Hubert Lucrecios is thinking of Caravaggio's *Narcissus*.

He's leafing though the *Chicago Tribune*, desperately looking for his letter, his note of indignation. For three days, he has been scanning the editorial pages, the letters to the editor, and hasn't found anything. The absence of his letter isn't discouraging him yet. He's sure that it will get published soon, pop up any day now.

So he muses about Caravaggio's *Narcissus*. Not the original painting, but its new iteration. Anyway, the version done by Vik Muniz, a contemporary artist who had a retrospective at the Art Institute of Chicago. Leafing frenetically through the thick newspaper, he notices an imposing ad, one of Caravaggio's paintings made out of junk, old computers, nuts, bolts, bicycle parts, car doors, dirty furniture, old prints. Inside a huge hangar, Muniz patiently assembled tons of scrap metal, steel, wood, and glass, transforming this heap of obsolete things into an image that unmistakably reproduced Caravaggio's painting.

How can anyone remain indifferent before this virtuosic assemblage?

How can anyone's words compete with such an eloquent work?

His letter will never get published, drowned in the flood of whiny letters sent to the *Tribune*. Does he still believe in it? Does he seriously want to get fired for making unkind comments against the company?

These questions are still floating around in his mind when there is a violent knock on the door.

A woman's familiar voice, a disagreeable, nasty voice, then more irritated knocks on the door.

What?

He stands up suddenly.

His first instinct is to wait. He holds up the phone, which he's picked up a bit absurdly. His index finger shakes above the automatic dial button for 911. Yet he hesitates. The knocks increase in volume. It's almost spooky. She'll soon break down the door by flinging herself at it.

Then comes an exchange of screams and abuse through the door.

The upstairs neighbour starts to bang on the floor when Lucrecios decides to open the door, threatening his impromptu visitor with the wooden handle of a broom.

As soon as Lucrecios appears in the doorframe, Christina Baldacci spits in his face.

* * *

Oprah arrives on the set, greeting the audience with a big hand movement. Satiara applauds without stopping, like a child intoxicated by respect.

Today's show is about the lives of happy, single people.

Oprah always welcomes her television viewers with a refined, effective message that's kind and precise. Camera two. She sits on her chic sofa. Camera three pans over the audience, Satiara appears immediately in the foreground.

Camera two. Close-up of Oprah's elastic face. It's the show's preamble, during which she reads the teleprompter and paints an honest portrait of happy, single people—a lively edit, interspersed with soft, graphic effects, busy curves, multiple fade in–fade outs—illustrating her topic, presenting happy, single people in different contexts.

Camera three. A wide shot of the audience. Camera two. Close-up of Oprah. Suspense. Why the wide shot of the audience?

Oprah asks the people in the audience who among them is

single and happy. Impossible to know. "Happy, single people are not that different from couples. You'll see," she says. The hypothesis that the show will try to prove has been made. Happy, single people are not different from happy couples. How so? The show will tell us.

Commercial break.

Satiara is glowing. This is her second time as an audience member of *The Oprah Winfrey Show*, and her excitement remains at an ecstatic high.

You have to reserve your ticket one month in advance. Then wait in line. Then follow the orders of the floor manager. Then not lose consciousness when the TV star comes on set.

For this young Cameroonian prostitute, Oprah is the queen mother of a benevolent planet. She reigns over a parallel universe where humiliation does not exist, where financial problems are miraculously solved thanks to the generous donations of charitable organizations, visionary benefactors, or humane detox centres run by Dr. Phil (Harpo Productions, founded by Oprah). Life is simple because Oprah loves us. From her office at 1058 Washington Boulevard, at the corner of Morgan, she governs an empire of love in Chicago.

Back to the show.

A segment on the invited guests.

Camera two. Medium-long shot of Oprah. She presents the first guest. An elegant man in his late thirties. A doctor. It's the typical portrait of an ideal single person. Responsible, charming, well-established—anyone with these qualities should not remain single. But it's Mark Winberger's choice.

A professional, quick montage of his daily life. We see him at work, in his doctor's lab coat, then at home with his dog, walking in the afternoon, then sitting alone at the table before a delicious-looking dish, gracefully handling knife and fork.

Camera two. Oprah makes a teasing joke. She announces that, what's more, he's an outstanding cook! Who wouldn't want him? She pouts, indicating all the attraction that a man of his calibre can generally arouse in women.

Camera three. Mark Winberger comes out from the wings. The floor manager indicates applause to the audience.

Satiara claps with gusto. Doesn't feel the tingling sensation, doesn't notice the redness of her palms. She's experiencing something extraordinary. She's experiencing an angelic interlude in her ordinary life. She doesn't blame anyone. She doesn't want to blame anybody. Men are what they are and she can't change them. But in the meantime, she can still dream, buy Beyoncé albums, and hang Oprah Winfrey posters in her small apartment.

One day, she will be a journalist for the *Chicago Tribune*, but for now, she has to pay the rent, pay for her American Lit courses, find a husband. But she doesn't want to find a husband right away. She understands people who make difficult choices or who can't do anything and allow themselves to be led by chance encounters. And she wants Mark Winberger to see her, to share the fullness of his life with a woman who has nothing.

She knows that Oprah would understand her, that Dr. Phil would find a way to cut through the passive mentality that rules her. She knows it, expects it, and that's enough. At

Harpo Studios, she's no longer a statistic; she's submerged in the desires of everyone. She becomes a *present* young woman. A young woman with dreams like everyone else.

Camera one. Mark Winberger explains that it's important to learn to live alone, whatever the cost. He seems to be preaching an extinct religion, a strange parable. With clear eloquence and simple phrases, he extols to the audience the importance of solitude, the importance of getting used to our solitary existence. In this respect, he points out that we dedicate at least half our lives to solitude, to moments of reflection, rest, solitary work, reading, watching, travel, silence, concentration, daydreams. Furthermore, others teach us how to accept our solitude better. They enable us to feel empathy, so as to better understand their own solitude. Community exists to help people accept their solitary fate. Helping another means giving them the means to better grasp their own singularity, their aloneness. Mark Winberger is not sad, he feels he's being logical. Camera two. Oprah looks at her guest, rolling her eyes. She tells him: "You have the temperament of a hermit!" We hear the audience laugh. Transition, montage.

Camera three. The floor manager asks for a warm applause to reward the guest's well-spoken remarks. Camera two. Oprah wonders whether happy, single people are not people who have been hurt in relationships, or embittered by mourning a lover.

The second part of the interview with Mark Winberger after the break.

Commercial break.

Satiara knows that we'll all end up like desiccated dogs, dead for days under the shrubs of the savannah. There's no

point in blaming life for anything. Liberated, affluent, humiliated, rich or poor, everyone will end up under some shrub,
eyes eaten by vultures, ribs licked by the wind, teeth exposed
to the sun, stripped of their rosy hue.

When she sees a client, she sees a desiccated dog. In the
moment, she even feels pity, clumsily tries to protect the men
she meets from their pathological solitude. Sometimes, she
kisses them, if she feels like it. Receives the other's distress
like a shameful gift.

Back to the show.

8.

PROSOPOPOEIA

GHISLAIN DIDN'T KNOW WHAT TO THINK ABOUT Courrège now. He had the impression that he wanted her. However, Maldonne was the one on his mind. But it came down to the same thing. He had no choice. He had nothing to reproach himself for. No one was asking him to take additional risks.

In his downtime, he couldn't help it, he thought of trivial things. He asked himself questions, analyzed his doubts by questioning his certainties.

In this manner, he examined his constitution as a reader, and considered himself the head of the department of lost paper.

He'd just seen a Norwegian film, *Reprise* by Joachim Trier. It tells the story of two budding writers and their relationship to success. One goes crazy, the other receives great acclaim for a difficult book called *Prosopopoeia*. Through a kind of *mise en abîme*, this formalist work reflects the film itself, conceived with a formal aesthetic reminiscent of the Honk Kong New Wave (choreographed action, stylized characters, sophisticated storyline, game of mirrors and echoes). A literary film delivering a story about brotherly friendship that turns to drama. Every community is built on tragedy, all fraternity conceals coarse jealousies. Friendship is a mental construct, an ideal. One sole person rejects this ideal, and the community dissolves, goes into crisis, breaks down. Those who can adapt the fastest will be the ones who will endure. Friendship is a house of cards abandoned to the winds. We all survive by changing, transforming, and losing friends.

Ghislain imagined a Quebecois literary success more phenomenal than *Harry Potter*. He could see those in the literary crowd—reticent, timid—devoting themselves to the sport of interviews, proliferating amusing comments, appearing at the international launch of the Quebecois book's English translation. Global media would invade Quebec's winter, straight-laced celebrities would wander around the city, Oprah Winfrey herself would come to record a special show in honour of *Prosopopoeia*'s author, live from the Lion d'Or one snowy night.[1]

---

[1] A crowd around the book table.

Oprah begins singing in English. Behind her, a PowerPoint slide show simultaneously transmits the French translation of her words. She sings in tune, handles the mic with confidence, puts on a show. Her brooding voice pierces through the general hubbub.

8. PROSOPOPOEIA

Prosopopoeia, whose title refers to a rhetorical device, would remind people that literature is ultimately only the vitalization of ideas in the form of hyperrealist stories or tales. All things considered, Ghislain entertained a somewhat hackneyed fantasy. But he delighted in how all of Quebec got a kick out of Céline Dion, who sanctioned any megalomaniacal behaviour, even the most idiotic. Besides, he believed that in a hundred years, Quebec's entire cultural and literary life of our time would be overshadowed by the rule of Céline Dion. In a hundred years, people would say "that was in Céline Dion's time." And they would have said all that there was to say about the cultural life of our era.

He couldn't help swallowing a smile of dazed satisfaction, a burgeoning laugh. His own era amused him, and this consoled him about everything. Even about his own futility as an ordinary reader.

That's when that he started thinking about Courrège.

He was looking for a banal loophole for his fleeting satisfaction.

He frittered away the rest of the day at the Grande Bibliothèque. He wanted to relax, get back to the books, camp in the ultimate readopolis.

Essentially, he wanted to assure himself that he was contributing to the world of print. And, by extension, to the world in general.

OPRAH'S SONG
(To the tune of Adamo's "C'est Ma Vie")

My story began with a few loving words
Mother reading me tales.

* * *

Maldonne was looking at the street while waiting for the bus. *Fade in–fade out. Interior shots of a Norwegian government helicopter. Dr. Larsen, the helmsman, the helicopter pilot, and Nicolas are onboard the small aircraft, flying just above the mountain peaks of the Magdalena Fjord. Hamlet's Twin.* Maldonne was brooding over the scene of

Often I gritted my teeth and dreamt of bliss.
I was a wise child.

Then came the day when I read my first book.
And was so transformed.

I then had the means to fill up with dreams,
My commonplace life.

Since then I've read thick novels,
Thrillers, short stories,
Works most profound.

Since then I've never confused
Beautiful dreams with night.
I'm happy just to laugh.

For some time
I wanted to impose
My ideal stories on the world.

But with the detectives of my senses close on my heels,
I chose to leave the ball.

REFRAIN
Prosopopoeia, prosopopoeia, I tell you my love of books, I live no better, I live no less than in your simple bliss.

Sylvie's disappearance. Her distressed lover, Nicolas Vanesse, goes to search for her.

Searching was an expiatory experience.

Searching buried philosophical contractions in a distant fjord, a strange country with the topography of an open book, karstic wounds, mythological valleys.

Curiously, Hubert Aquin was sometimes seen as a philosophical writer. This didn't fit his persona of a postmodern

Onstage, the notes fly over the murmur of the room. Oprah sways with remarkable vigour. Everyone is happy.

Everyone participates in the carnival of the famished. It is winter if not summer. The shyest of the shy versify in the darkness, beers in hand.

Oprah shouts out "Bonjour Montreal!" before carrying on.

All the cameras of the United States follow this singing allegory on two legs who is presenting a novelistic allegory in the guise of a final outburst for a new novel. Thank you to our sponsors.

André Roy is delighted. He gently nudges Francis Farley-Chevrier, who usually avoids group celebrations. They are at the entrance of the Lion d'Or. All of Montreal's literati are there. The thirsty, the neurotics, the followers, the temperamentals, and the Slovaks. André Roy is delighted. He talks of a historic moment, and everyone agrees with him.

Today, the arts cavalry is galloping in unison. All those in the Montreal world of letters are stamping on the floor of the Lion d'Or. Fernand Durepos makes a few vague remarks to Jean-Sébastien Larouche, monsieur *Dacnomanie*. Nearby, Robbert Fortin pats the head of Tristan Malavoy's young son. The party has begun. Jean-François Poupart, just coming in, greets Jean-Marc Desgent, who's following him. Jean-Marc is holding Annie Darveau's hand. No one lingers at the door. Jean-Paul Daoust, more fit than an Iron Man, pops in, making a funny comment.

Sitting at the first table, a lustful and tender Benoît Chaput thinks of a retort, while Éric de Larochellière gives his caustic opinion on the state of Quebec letters.

Daniel Canty is lost in thought, musing on *Alice* and his ongoing translation of Stephanie Bolster, while also getting some new ideas for Marie Brassard's pioneer. Nevertheless, the scene where the character of Nicolas Vanesse goes in search of Sylvie, his "daughter of fire," in the forgotten corners of the Svalbard archipelago always plunged her into an embarrassing post-romantic reverie.

Her romantic liver throbbed in her concentrated body. She was digesting the strange toxins of Aquin's post-romantic images with unusual compunction.

Waiting for the bus was an expiatory experience. Surveying the city with strangers and a driver too at ease to be polite

Peepshow (he's her dramaturgy consultant). Another Daniel, the American Daniel C. Dennett, is busy discussing his new book, *Sweet Dreams: A Philosophy of Mindfulness and Somaesthetics*, with the young philosopher-to-be, Erik Bordeleau.

Hanging back, with a luminous face and mischievous eyes, Oana Avasilichioaei waves to Erín Moure so that she spots her through the crowd. A consummate multi-tasker, the young poet/one-woman-orchestra is jotting down a scene set in a Vancouver park while playing with the cocktail umbrella of her neon-green drink.

Smiling back at a persuaded reader, emboldened by the success of his new novel *How to Become a Monster*, Jean Barbe still feels some unease before this literary display of sequins and glitter. Meanwhile, a few metres away at the bar, Perrine Leblanc orders a lemon Perrier.

Steve Savage never strays far from his pretty girlfriend. Alain Farah, who doesn't get out much, is talking about meeting Olivier Cadiot. David Leblanc listens while Geneviève Gravel-Renaud leaves to find a chair. There's a lack of chairs, and all these lovely people are leaning on the venue's north wall. Near the stage, during Oprah's long comical tremolo, Claude Beausoleil purses his lips politely at Yolande Villemaire, who is concentrating on the vocalizations of the hostess.

Near the northernmost central column, Robert Giroux and François Hébert seem to appreciate their grey hair, each with a champagne glass in hand, found who knows where, while next to them Raymond Martin is talking with Marie-Hélène Montpetit, flanked by Éric McComber.

But the show wouldn't be the same without Pierre Ouellet, Paul Bélanger, and Philippe Beck hiding in a corner near the washrooms, debating a specific aspect of William Carlos Williams's work.

At the same moment when the familiar refrain of Adamo's song distorts the air, Stéphane Despatie takes Corinne Chevarier's hand, slightly brushing

annoyed her. She thought again of Micheline Lanctôt's film, *Sonatine*, of Pascale Bussières and Marcia Pilote fishing for amity from bus drivers and people on the subway. Maldonne feared the reassuring solitude of public transportation, the sliding doors and terrible, gravedigger ticket clerks, their notorious impatience (which secretly meant go, quickly, get swallowed up, go, there are others besides you to bury today). But what was feeding her melancholy? What was its basis? Not Ghislain, anyway?

her right breast. Everybody at the bar pretends not to be looking at them. Attentive yet dissolute, Maxime Catellier, beer in hand, bends over backwards telling Shawn Cotton an anecdote about Burroughs. The bar is full. Samuel Beckett sips an amaretto sour while saying something to Charles Bolduc, whom no one recognizes.

Nadine Bismuth is standing by the emergency exit, taping her foot to the music. She kisses Yves P. Pelletier, who imitates Stromgol for about three seconds before taking off in search of a martini. Carole David, wearing a long cape, avoids Yves Boisvert, who in turn avoids Chrystine Brouillet. Boisvert will get his due; he'll be speaking in Russian by the end of the evening. People are bustling around the book table. A book of tunes. Call-and-response songs, magazines, novels.

Hands buying, hands touching books, hands leafing through pages. Gaëtan Lévesque and Éric Blackburn grab money, give back change, offer up several copies of a book that only exists in the minds of this novel's readers from a box under the table. No one is safe from fakes, and if any slaps arise, Gaëtan Lévesque will be the one collecting them on his florid cheeks.

On the south side of the room, rows of tables, people, conversations merge in the general chaos.

Pierre Lefebvre and Olivier Kemeid broadcast sharp grunts, which Karine Hubert is translating. Two days later, she will transform this performance into a poem about digestion. At the same table, Louis-Jean Thibault sends a text to his radiologist girlfriend. Then everyone hears Mistral's thundering voice, as she's laughing near the entrance and farting like Tiberius, drowning out Oprah, who's just finishing her song. Mistral then grabs her friend Kevin by the shoulders and says: "This woman is more influential than Bush and Obama put together!" Kevin's girlfriend smiles and nods.

Lost in a halo of stage lighting, Gaëtan Dostie is documenting the whole

No.

Ah, maybe yes.

Actually, she hadn't the faintest idea.

The bus showed up at the time indicated in the timetable. No one noticed anymore that this was a small miracle. No one noticed anymore the dozens of urban miracles that are the foundation of contemporary life. No one noticed anymore the young preoccupied women in glass bus shelters, gently bobbing their heads, isolated by music.

event, his camera practically invisible. At the back of the room, Pierre Nepveu is talking in a low voice with Gilles Marcotte, who never goes out, but who is there today, visibly irritated by all the hubbub. Myriam Brunelle takes the opportunity to ask Nepveu a question. This isolated table resembles a peaceful clearing in a wild wood.

At the next table, Martine Audet is watching the show with interest, while tenderly sneaking glances at Catherine Mavrikakis, who is taking notes in a spiral notebook. Hanging back but keyed up, Mathieu Arsenault and Marie-Hélène Cabana give each other ironic glances every time Oprah addresses the audience to praise the merits of the nonexistent book. Thierry Dimanche, just back from the bar, is describing his mycological escapade to Annie Lafleur, who is flanked on her left by Renée Gagnon, dressed in black lace and sporting a sexy nose ring.

In the middle of the room, a dozen tables complete the set. At a table in the back, Geneviève Letarte and José Acquelin are discussing the Banff studios, while Louis Hamelin and Patrice Desbiens drink blond beer and talk up great American authors. In his straw hat, Patrick Poulin is making a paper boat while Marc-Antoine K. Phaneuf is writing two poems at a table, thinking of Philippe Charron and David Duchovny.

At a table near the central aisle, which divides the room in two, Franz Schürch is recounting a poker feat to Alexandre Laferrière and Pascal-Angelo Fioramore. Claudine Vachon walks towards the entrance, stepping over Mélanie Vincelette's feet, who starts a conversation with Éric Dupont, fascinated by Oprah's professionalism.

Suzanne Myre doesn't dare go into the Lion d'Or and instead waves at Mélanie Vincelette from a distance, remains frozen by the awe-inspiring aura of the North American alpha female who has deigned to visit the people living north of the forty-fifth parallel. It's historic, entertaining, and already kitsch.

8. PROSOPOPOEIA

No one would have the patience to sympathize with everyone's problems, everyone's doubts, everyone's stories, everyone's melancholic whims, everyone's unsaid words. No one can really attest to it, but everyone knows that we all have three secret thoughts for every one thought revealed. Who notices the size of the iceberg beneath the civil level of conversation? When a telepathic Google comes into existence, half the planet will cry out of spite the first time they access others'

She lets Claudine Vachon enter and goes back outside to soothe her brain, aching from the public heat.

The usual outsiders are standing outside the Lion d'Or—Alexandre Faustino, Jean-Philippe Bergeron, Véronique Marcotte—reading the menu of a Turkish pizza place. Everyone is having fun. Tania Langlais, Kim Doré, and Geneviève Blais take note of a pasta recipe with artichokes and cream, narrated by the languorous voice of Guillaume Vigneault, who's just stepped out of his military Cessna. The road is closed off, the security cordon has made amateur photographers pop up everywhere, who snap headshots, coerce hearts, shove faces. A thirteen-year-old photographer catches Nicolas Dickner looking away from the lens, seemingly absorbed by an amusing thought or two about Kurt Vonnegut. Nearby, Antoine Tanguay is talking at length with Sébastien Chabot about the village of Sainte-Souffrance.

Even the great ancients come to haunt them. Ronfard, Aquin, Ferron, Basile, La Rocque, Bessette, and Gabrielle Roy jump out of taxis, run down the street, then liquefy on the sidewalks. A messy ballet that provokes some nervous laughter. Tania Langlais tries to collect some of Aquin's mush, quickly freezing in the galvanized winter. Nothing remains in liquid form too long. Only Huguette Gaulin doesn't freeze, liquefying the black ice around her.

Back inside, Oprah introduces Denis Villeneuve, who will host the rest of the evening: a dance floor, a cancan, and a chorus of masseuses will be coming up. It's a chance for the dancers to wake up. Roger Des Roches shakes his hips and moves his mane, Lucie Bélanger follows his pelvic movements. Ollivier Dyens and Elsa Pépin take the opportunity to leap to the dance floor. Spinning with studied, characteristic slowness near the edge, Louis Gauthier mixes into the fray despite himself.

Violaine Forest and Marie Hélène Poitras shake their inner children, arms raised to the ceiling. Stéphane Dompierre and Patrick Brisebois push the rest

thoughts and problems. People will hold back from thinking too much. No doubt, a few years later, thoughts will start being taxed.

* * *

Arriving at the Grande Bibliothèque, Ghislain ran right into Courrège, who was working at the information coun-

of the tables and chairs to the side to make room for more dancers. Behind the mixing console, Mélika Abdelmoumen is having a tête-à-tête with Olivier Choinière, reminiscing about Serge Doubrovsky.

The chorus of masseuses hijacks the stage and commandeers Pascal Assathiany's participation, as he happens to be passing by for some unknown reason. Michel Vézina raises his hand and joins the masseuses, lifts his legs, notes the moves of the energetic artists. Maxime-Olivier Moutier, Robert Soulières, and Bernard Pozier join the line, hold on to waists, mumbling the tune, mimicking the beat.

Stanley Péan, who is entertaining a group of writers composed of Corinne Larochelle, Jean-Pierre Girard, Élise Turcotte, and Andrée A. Michaud, suddenly takes out his trumpet and blares thirds and fourths, accompanies the backing vocalists at the high pitch of their notes.

Back in the hall leading to the washrooms, Simon Dumas toasts glasses with Brigitte Malenfant as they exchange notes about their experiences in Mexico. Jean-Éric Riopel listens to Clara Brunet-Turcotte, lets Aimée Verret pass by, accompanied by Bertrand Laverdure, who seems to be in hurry to return to the stage and the chorus of masseuses. Verret stops midway, stunned to meet a guitarist from New York, and loses interest in the general atmosphere.

Oprah comes back onstage and takes up her refrain, talks about her foundation, her schools in Africa, introduces the book that does not exist to a crowd straight out of a B-movie starring Donald Pilon. The music raises arms and pounds temples.

Guillaume Corbeil is having fun playing pétanque in the dirty snow with Christian Bök. Louise Bouchard and François Charron mutually offer to hang up each other's coats. Michael Delisle gets himself a Diet Coke at the bar, whispers a few volatile words to his companion, Lise Tremblay, who is drinking

ter on the second floor. They each noticed surprise in the other's gestures. They began a conversation in Morse code, intercut by short and long breaths. A tacit handbook regulated the type of conversations allowed at work. Thirty years of talk shows, soap operas, intellectual comedies, TV series, sitcoms, shocking interviews, MTV, online chats, blogs, and YouTube had constructed modes of interpersonal interaction. You had to be self-depreciating, never take

a Long Island Iced Tea with two straws. At the same moment, the bartender drops a bunch of change into her already ample tip jar.

A discernible René Lapierre appears at the back of the stage, whispers a few words to Benoit Jutras and Maude Smith Gagnon, then withdraws to more thoroughly liquefy on the sidewalk outside. Telescopic poems surge up in the darkness, Paul Chamberland pops up around the corner and inhales the formidable odour of the heathen mass electrifying the multitude.

In the vestibule, Nicole Brossard finishes her scotch, scratches her solar plexus, sniffs a bit. The crowd has spilled over; Denise Desautels drinks her pastis with remarkable presence, as Paul Chanel Malenfant walks over to his two friends, holding his scarf and blowing his nose.

Outside, Brigitte Caron and Serge Lamothe start talking about sex, surprise themselves, describe their urges in detail: polyamorous relationships and tales of Laval. New friendships, frequent and bracing encounters.

On three distinct, yellow snowmobiles, Pierre Labrie, Carl Lacharité, and Mario Brassard steer between the guests, for various practical reasons, establish pathways, race up Ontario Street, take Gaston Bellemare home.

The chorus of masseuses now comes down from the stage into the room, leads the resistant and the unadventurous into an awkward farandole. People rise from the tables, laugh, show signs of depravation, signals of amusing distress. They pray a little (Ouellette, Fréchette), they drink a lot (everyone else). It's thirst *avant la lettre*. Hands and plastic forks descend upon the long buffet, elegantly laid out behind the book table. Bernard Andrès tries the gouda; Bertrand Gervais swallows a no-crust, egg salad sandwich; André Vanasse and André Carpentier catch some of the canapés flitting about at the whim of the paths taken by a few designated waiters sporting bowties and linen vests. Simon Harel grabs a mini-goat cheese quiche, exchanges a concentrated look with Jonathan Lamy, who is holding Catherine Cormier-Larose's hand, her-

yourself seriously, never swagger, never doubt the validity of urban life.

Ghislain was neither funny (at least not intentionally) nor threatening, so he had no choice. He had to keep it brief. Not drag on too long. In one of Molière's or Racine's plays, a character like Ghislain would have played the minor role of a maidservant or a confidante. The plays had receptacles for confidences and dischargers of confidences. Despite his

self stunned by a sudden movement—Oprah's stumbling for a moment before standing straight again. Agitation in the room, everything is suddenly extinguished then lit up again as soon as the hostess in a trance regains her balance. Some grit their teeth. Sylvie Bérard bursts out laughing. Denise Brassard and Francis Catalano walk against the tide, take advantage of the general confusion to work their way towards Stéphane Despatie and Corinne Chevarier, still at the back of the bar, now entwined.

In front of the mixing console, between the bar and a stool, Dominique Robert and Léon Guy Dupuis are talking to each other. Pierre Samson is waiting for his Bloody Caesar at the bar. Martin-Pierre Tremblay toasts with Tony Tremblay.

At last, the moment of needless repetition comes. Oprah, excited, electrified by her own radiant energy, tells the crowd: "Keep it up! Always keep it up!" Then sings the evening's official song for a second time, the ode to the health of the book, the ballad of all happy readers.

Prosopopoeia. Prosopopoeia. Today, we launch a novel. A book about a parrot and so much more.

You watch the film on which all novels will be based once again. A film about perdition. You see yourself straying off the beaten path. Only you've lost your pole.

We kiss at the back of the classroom while reading our songs. It's a great benefit. A novel, you know, is only a line through reason.

The masseuses seek out the eyes of single people, imitate the ardour of the stars in a Walt Disney cartoon.

They forget to frown, speak in soft and loud voices, dissect the contemporary trends passing under everyone's nose. Walking between the tables with his

8. PROSOPOPOEIA

propensity to philosophize, Ghislain did not possess the verve of protagonists, new TV stars, instant celebrities. He accepted this.

Raphaëlle de Groot had not been satisfied with leaving her bookplate only in Gombrowicz's book. She had left her trace in a multitude of books.

boom microphone, Thomas Braichet records the disconnect between goods and people. Brandishing mics, Catherine Perrin and the *Flash* team wait impatiently in the wings for Oprah to be free, as Louis Cornellier, Christian Desmeules, and Michel Lapierre scribble notes while standing near the entrance, chatting up the ticket clerk. Everyone's having the time of their lives. Jean-François Nadeau and Nadia Roy evoke a trip to the States by mentioning Amherst and Emily Dickinson. The vestibule is now full. It's a mob scene. Hugues Corriveau brushes against David Cantin.

Ook Chung and Yong Chung are discussing games and Amélie Nothomb. The outer door is jammed. With their elbows on the cloakroom counter, Robert Lévesque and Stéphane Lépine debate a detail of Thomas Bernhard's life. Danielle Laurin is trying to catch Hélène Dorion to ask her for an interview.

François Couture spits out an olive pit while shaking Jon Paul Fiorentino's hand. At the back of the room, the lighting engineer, an older Marie-Paule with sparkling eyes, shakes everyone's hand. To the side, Isabelle Courteau is talking with Louise Dupré, a glass of wine in her hand.

Fifty rowdy students swell the aisles, pull up their sleeves.

Nancy R. Lange braves the careful silence of Jean-Sébastien Huot, who is trying Carl Lacharité's snowmobile. Outside, it's snowing. Inside, a head wind is blowing. They use body language. No one laughs without reason anymore; they spy on each other without knowing it, complying with the acrobatics of punishment, slightly afraid of the Dany Laferrière inside them, who scolds while laughing, then takes out a small leather whip and taps the backside of Jacques Godbout, who quickly walks away towards René-Daniel Dubois, talking with Robert Lalonde at a table. They're trying to outdo each other with cleverness to mark this historic moment, worthy of the sulphurous nights of Sylvain Trudel, who is absent as usual. Saul Bellow is also missing in action. The portrait photographer is missing a model.

When I saw Ghislain. When he extricated me from a long moment of inattention, I divulged my discovery; I told him about the latest result of my de Grootian excavations.

The artist had stuck a bookplate in one of Saul Bellow's books, the translation of *More Die of Heartbreak*, whose approximate French title was *Le cœur à bout de souffle*. This was ex libris number 105. The book's call number was 813.54 B448co. The date "October 3, 1998" was stamped on the book. A text, always the same, in typewriter type, framed

Ghislain doesn't know where to wander anymore, whom to greet; he thinks about Oprah's song, his education as a reader, the enormous relief awaiting him once this novel is finished. It's crazy what one must endure to feel human. In the heat of the moment, Courrège kisses him on the cheek and hugs him close, while letting out a fraternal sigh.

Who is right, the reader or the writer?

Ghislain closes his eyes to stop thinking. The end is near.

A radiant reader, Sophie Asselin, thanks him, praises his insight, and makes him want to reproduce.

Forty-nine new authors pass through the Lion d'Or, build networks, believe in the added value of their works. Sixty partiers launch into a street song with seven choir singers-masseuses who hurry to the middle of the room. Everyone loves doubly and drinks doubles.

Everyone accepts the common space while quibbling about the commonness of others. Everyone hides their game. No one's heard Gilles Archambault, or Louis-Philippe Hébert, or Pierre-A. Larocque (with good reason: the last one is dead). The absent ones turn into ice cubes that the others palm off in their thoughts in the fridge of quotations. Everyone is playing pin the tail on the donkey. No one wears a blindfold; open-eyed, they make out the ears and dunce's caps.

Little by little, Ghislain loses his sense of self. Knocking back the booze, he goes to look for a chair in the middle of the Lion d'Or. No chair is free. Courrège searches with him, and they plunder glasses in the process.

The road to the chair is long. In a skullcap, Hervé Bouchard accompanies them with his six orphans.

Behind the stage curtain, they find a gimpy, three-legged chair.

Ghislain balances his buttocks on the chair, engages his muscles in a dance of restraint.

8. PROSOPOPOEIA

the unusual bookplate on the left side: "Everywhere, on every book of this library, you leave your fingerprints over those of the previous readers. Together with the others, you form a skin on every work without realizing it."
A skin of sorrow, without a doubt.

Courrège sinks to the ground, exhausted. A fog of beer in her eyes, Oprah's voice in her right eardrum.
Ghislain, a clown on three legs, says to Courrège, who is somewhat stupefied by the evening:
—That's it! I'm taking a rest!
Tomorrow, a thousand other people will crowd in.
Proud of his comical timing that falls a bit flat, he repeats:
—That's it! I'm taking a rest!

9.

PLATO'S OCTAHEDRON

STYLE.
Life style.
Style kills.
Style doesn't kill.
Style dictates and retracts.
It is an animal, a machine, a new virus or a morbid algorithm.

Lucrecios was running in circles in his confusion. Lucrecios wrote to let it out, then dragged his clumsy phrases into the trash and clicked on *Empty trash*. Tapped, clicked, emptied.

He was dead. Clinically speaking. A fluorescein eye stain test. A dilated fundus examination. Nothing worked.

What had happened to him? What had he attempted?

He needed to forget. Do anything to forget. He needed to erase himself, cross himself out, find some support to bear his new life.

He limped. Style kills, then flees. Style answers, destroys, and disappears.

Time to stop. Display of boors.

Night of forgiveness. Red carpet night. Cold night deprived of autumn.

* * *

The architect didn't complain about people who vanished anymore. His circle of friends resembled a geometric line that was becoming blurry. Less points, more vague.

How many have been worn down by the accumulation of various frustrations? Roger, the poor character in Douglas Coupland's novel *The Gum Thief*, asked himself this universal question: Why am I me instead of another?

Everyone experiences a moment of dissatisfaction at a certain age.

Psychologists have terms to describe this impasse, as do anthropologists, also "influential" astrologers and scientists. This impasse is evident, shared, reassuring, because it strengthens us in our common humanity.

No one is ever at ease, no one is ever completely satisfied. Satisfaction kills.

Satisfaction doesn't deserve eulogies. It drives out inventiveness and indulges habits. Why would Greengrass be angry at Lucrecios for giving him the silent treatment for more than a month and a half? Greengrass's determination had been transformed into respectful waiting. Three unanswered phone calls and two forays into Barnes & Noble had convinced him. Lucrecios's silhouette didn't lie. It attested to his presence at work. He seemed well. His secret expedition completed, Greengrass had decided to withdraw into his territory and wait.

Sooner or later, Lucrecios would think of him, dial his number, send him a funny text, a few words to repair the damage, deny the possibility of disaster.

In the meantime, Greengrass spent time with his friend Pete. A shy office clerk, an old high school classmate, a bullied guy metamorphosed into a grey-carpet cockroach, a silent-elevator user, a reader of all the *Star Wars* books, a Bears fan of the Fritos Jalapeño Cheddar Cheese Dip–type.

Friendship crosses through Alice's looking glass and tells us of our infinitude.

There is no recipe for tolerating amicable panic. You just need to train, read a bit more, and take advantage of loopholes, available at anytime.

Cable television friendship. Wi-Fi friendship.

* * *

The video interface.

The rectangle of the Lumière brothers. The new mini-television that's turned on by clicking on a triangular button. The imperceptible wait for the upload.

Lucrecios had had enough. He stamped his feet with impatience. He wanted his life to change. Communicating was no longer an adequate word. He wanted all the cameras in the world to reassure him.

The Official Wizard of Books would become a famous website.

He would create his own literary quiz.

He had waited for others all his life.

He had the impression that life was made up of periods of pain alternating with points of growth. Each period involved a painful experience followed by a sensible solution. Pain then sense. Pain then response. Pain then transformation. The system was as ordered as musical staff paper, but it seemed to him that it leaned more towards pain these days.

And anyway, what is friendship if not a valve?

With a Styrofoam cross on the back, a friend walks us to Golgotha, relives with us the pre- and post-pain moments, but only as an echo. Friends are mimes. They duplicate our difficulties and reproduce our fears. They're a cave in which to project our inner life. Changing friends means changing what you see. Congratulations, you have new friends! Friendship can be bought; friendship can be exchanged; friendship is the material of change.

On credit, he bought a digital camera, a tripod, Final Cut Pro, some spotlights, and transformed a corner of his bedroom into a game show set.

This is what he deserved, new skin. He was going to invest in *his* community.

Fucking stiffness of everything besides the light of translucid communication, fuck that and fuck y'all!

He set off on a crusade. He had had enough.

Fucking white low-lifes, fucking drug lords, fucking gansta gold maniacs, fucking NASCAR drivers, fucking Brazilian billionaire, fucking cunt, fucking midget with attitude, fucking government that chokes truth and treats us like Daffy Duck in a cheap cartoon, fucking think-tank, fucking Arnold Schwarzenegger, fucking Chicago tourists, fucking friends that say nothing else but the official line, fucking nihilists, fucking rainbow-tainted optimists, fucking people who kill themselves for nothing but to escape their cheap and painful inner souls, fucking impatient bastard, fucking pity. Fuck love that bullies everything it touches and fuck luck, good or bad, and fuck Oprah's stupid kindness and fuck everyone who cries for you and fuck you, Christina.

* * *

B.A.L.D.A.C.C.I., a chic handbag brand.

* * *

She had decided. The plan wasn't working anymore. The men no longer managed to secrete the silvering of the mirror. Everything showed, the wings offstage, the ugliness, the frumpy production of the matrix. Everything oozed.

She thought of the word "shimmering," and imagined death like a fabric on which to stretch out.

With her whole body, she hoped. With her whole body, she was done with the dramatics of men in Mercedes (Porsches or Audis) or in Cubs (Bears or Giants) caps. She hoped for an abstract rain, for death and calm.

She would have liked to end like Harold Washington, struck down by a heart attack on his desk. But first she needed to solve her last puzzle, to insert the remaining piece that would complete her image. You can only die once the game is finished.

She thought of Lucrecios, of the paradoxical hate she had hoarded in order to unleash it on him one day.

Once you exit life and the game is over, there's no better piece to fill the void than the one bearing a failed love.

Before succumbing to the terminal rage that would liberate her, she would empty herself, like you do when pissing, of her poison. And she would make sure to adjust the last piece of her puzzle, whatever the cost, even if she had to strike it with a hammer like a madwoman to make all the angles of her hate fit in the hole of her incomplete image, before her disappearance.

And then?

Nothing.

It would be over, period.

* * *

Greengrass was drinking alone, poisoning his liver.

A friend from the third zone. A so-called vague acquaintance. Had told him.

At Jimmy's Woodlawn Tap, at noon.

That Christina Baldacci had killed herself.

* * *

Her throat was pissing blood (a bleeding sow) after the cut with the X-Acto.

Just beforehand, she had watched Oprah Winfrey's special show at Auschwitz with Elie Wiesel, over and over. Christina became enraged and excited, but not for the right reasons. She knew that she would soon take action. But she waited in stupid infamy for the Christian flow of human tears. She cried because you had to cry, and raged because she no longer had the energy to be indignant. For her, Primo Levi was the one, not the saccharine, moralizing Wiesel. She followed Levi and cried for the periodic table.

Playboy was founded in Chicago. Hefner was Mr. Chicago. Nelson Algren had spit in his soup after agreeing to come to one of Hefner's parties. *Playboy* meant luxury, fame. *Playboy* resembled de Sade's castle, but without the scandalous marquis. The hallways still held fear, but only in order to uphold a waning myth.

Algren dreaded what he called "the third person society." The false distance that encourages excess in all its forms, artificial values, and all the Hugh Hefners. Algren died penniless. Oprah would have invited him on her show, if he hadn't died on May 9, 1991, before it was created. Oprah is today's Simone de Beauvoir. Algren is the one who wrote letters that no one read to the French author that all women claim to have read. You only hear of love for Beauvoir. Baldacci didn't write, but could imagine letters to infinite correspondents.

During the ad for a vinaigrette low in aerosol, she would kill herself.

Her last earthly show: a healthy woman of the Martha Stewart variety frugally spraying some vinaigrette.

* * *

Algren showed the concrete implications of the values *Playboy* propagated, by creating a character who appears, on several occasions, in the Algrenian corpus. He is called Rhino Gross in *A Walk on the Wild Side* and Dingdong Daddy in *The Last Carousel*. He reigns in the sterile and claustrophobic world of O'Daddyland, a repugnant condom factory, and appears to be a transparent incarnation of Hugh Hefner. Algren puts words in his mouth that are practically identical to those spoken by the *Playboy* owner, reproduced in *Who Lost an American?* and based on an interview in the *Wall Street Journal*:

"'I'm in the happy position,' he announced like a man running for office, 'of becoming a legend in my own time! I have everything I ever wanted! Success in business! Identity as an individual!'" (Dindong in *The Last Carousel* 51)

"'I'm in the happy position of becoming a living legend in my own time,' Hefner said, 'I have everything I ever wanted—success in business and identity as an individual!'" (*Who Lost an American?* 300)

Rhino Gross tirelessly spews out the same philosophy as Tom O'Connor:

"Look out for love, look out for trust, look out for *giving*. Look out for wine, look out for daisies and people who laugh readily. Be especially wary of friendship, Son, it can lead only to trouble." (*A Walk on the Wild Side* 181)

The entire credo of the third person society is exposed here; abstaining from all relationships with others is the only way to guarantee happiness. Gross lives in a schizophrenic world, cut off from the city and nature, immersed in a reddish-brown fog because of the rubber, the quintessential industrial material and a symbol of the particularly profitable creations of "business." The condom rubber contaminates everything, even the taste of food, and transforms the employees-prisoners into mutants, such as Velma, turned "the Vulcanized Woman" (177). While the overlord may well be a repellent individual, on the margins of respectable society, he is nonetheless representative of the middle class due to his professional success.

Rhino Gross is the creator of O'Daddy condoms; like Hefner, he owes his professional success to the industrial exploitation of his clients' erotic urges. In contrast to the *Playboy* owner, however, his fortune doesn't alleviate the spite he harbours against the human species, whose reproduction he successfully labours to curb. He believes that the origin of his problems coincides with the origin of life itself, and logically finds in his misogyny an outlet for his discontent.

Frédéric Dumas, "Éros est mort à Chicago: Nelson Algren accuse *Playboy*,"* https://erea.revues.org/92?lang=en.

* * *

To: readmeagain@sympatico.ca
From: earnestoearnesto@gmail.com

Hey Ghis!

Have you seen the new game!?

Gone on Book Wizard lately?

Lucrecios is black, did you know? We see him in the preamble. He explains how the game works. It's a game of predictions, an update of his initial idea, ultimately.

---

* "Eros Is Dead in Chicago: Nelson Algren Blames *Playboy*" (Trans.)

Do you have *Dungeons & Dragons*? We can use that to play his new game.

He wants us to use eight-sided dice, octahedrons. He explains that they're among Plato's perfect polyhedrons, perfect shapes that described the world, according to the philosopher. I didn't fully understand his English allusions to the migration of isosceles and scalene triangles. In any case, he claims that he didn't invent any of it, he stole it all from *Timaeus*, a dialogue I don't know... He also said—this I understood and found the metaphor amusing—that each of these perfect polyhedrons is associated with an original earthly element. The octahedron is the wind. The cube is the earth. Fire is the dodecahedron.

A die of wind is sweet, I think.

If you don't have octahedron dice, you can use paper, eight scraps of paper that you pick out of a hat or cone.

The game is simple. You just need to pick three times or roll the die three times. Each time, we're looking for one thing, one item of information. Once we randomly combine the three items of information needed, we can then predict the title of a future book and add this prediction to the list on his site.

I'll explain. We first roll the die to determine what type of writer will write our book. Secondly, to find which literary genre interests the writer; and thirdly, to discover the tenor of the book to be published, and the quality of the writing.

9. PLATO'S OCTAHEDRON

Lucrecios has provided values for each of the die's eight digits. I'll give them to you, but you can also go to the site to see them.

So here are the values of each digit, or rather, the descriptions corresponding to each one:

For the first roll, the types of writers:

1 – experimental
2 – mainstream
3 – scholarly
4 – careerist
5 – bad
6 – precious
7 – award-winning
8 – professional

For the second roll, the types of work and/or literary genre:

1 – nonfiction
2 – whodunit
3 – horror
4 – historical novel
5 – literary novel
6 – romance
7 – how-to book
8 – poetry

And for the third roll, the tenor of the books in question:

1 – first work
2 – mature work
3 – transitional work
4 – potboiler
5 – insignificant work
6 – failure
7 – scandalous work
8 – masterpiece

For example, if I roll a *two* to start, then a *four*, and lastly a *seven*, I must predict the next work of a mainstream writer, who writes historical novels, and who will launch a scandalous book in the next few months.

As a result, I could predict that James Michener will start writing *Iraq: The True War*, a thick polemical brick on the recent history of this derelict country, and this, without giving way when it comes to describing the collateral cruelty inflicted on the Iraqi people by the American contingent.

Of course, it's impossible. But I would have the right to post this prediction on the *Wizard of Books*.

The thrill of the game is that you have to react quickly, in front of the camera. It's the live performance aspect that gives the prediction exercise an element of game-show-like feverishness...

9. PLATO'S OCTAHEDRON

At best, we'll have a lot of fun with this new setup; at worst, we'll be a laughingstock. Part of the joy of TV-web game shows is to make fun of the hosts or contestants.

Courrège
xx

* * *

MALDONNE: What do you think of Chicago?

PASCAL: I've got nothing against it.

MALDONNE: It's the city of *Wizard of Books*...

PASCAL: Ah, that book prediction trivia... That's still interesting you all?

MALDONNE: Why "you all"?

PASCAL: Hasn't Ghislain infected everyone?

MALDONNE: *Infected*?

PASCAL: Your illness. Your book obsession. Real conjunctivitis.

MALDONNE: It keeps you on your game.

PASCAL: Ghislain just has to speak and he gives me conjunctivitis.

MALDONNE: The guy who runs the site is from Chicago. He's just set up a new video interface.

PASCAL: Wow, the geek literary narcissism is terrifying.

MALDONNE: How's that?

PASCAL: Truth is a fancy whore.

MALDONNE: You make me sick when you get on your high horse.

PASCAL: I hate cultured trendiness, I can't help it.

MALDONNE: Ah, you're pissing me off.

She leaves Pascal's apartment forgetting to slam the door. End of scene.

* * *

Ghislain gave back the change to an old woman buying some Lipton chicken noodle soup.

A lineup. When it was more than three people long, he always heard feet shuffling on the floor, quiet sighs. The impatient ones had the gift of making him sick. The gross outrage at having to wait for two brief minutes for a pack of Excel Extreme Fuse gum, a pack of Du Maurier Extra Light cigarettes, and a loaf of Gadoua 100% enriched white bread. They grumbled for a Doritos Cool Ranch, a Mars dark/noir bar, New and Improved/Nouveau et amélioré, and 500 ml of Pfanner Lemon Lychee juice.

He would have liked to yawn, open his mouth, wolf down the 99,367 products of the dep and survive, film the mastication and ingestion that would take a year, then stream it on UbuWeb.

In front of a Chinese client buying a Belgian beer, he thought of the last film of the Korean Park Chan-wook. He would have liked to hire him to direct *I'm a Cyborg But That's Okay*, with him as the main character. He liked martial arts expressions and military metaphors: *Clean it up*. In films, when someone "cleaned" with weapons, it was always much messier afterwards. Military clean-up was a false clean-up; they messed things up royally to satisfy a sort of really cool anal fantasy.

* * *

Lucrecios rejoiced. Three times more visits. His video clips were popular.

He didn't rejoice anymore when he thought of Baldacci. As soon as he turned away from the screen and noticed the presence of a Chicago parrot, tears came to his eyes. Why had Christina done it?

Lucrecios was tormented.

But now he was receiving congratulations, cheerful and encouraging emails. He needed them. It slightly paralyzed him to attract so many comments from strangers. It amused him because it was an avenue that thwarted the "whys." Any avenue that thwarted the "whys" seemed good to him, useful.

The fatal stupidity of a nihilist wasn't going to screw up his life. The tears and questions weren't for him, not now.

* * *

Ghislain frantically sent out a prank JPEG about the launch of *Prosopopoeia* to his list of friends. Nothing subtle about it. A few lines, suspiciously laudatory, and the name of a fake publishing house to top it off. Ultimately ridiculous, but he thought he was being tolerably funny.

He even sent it to Lucrecios, who added it to his scrolling banner. How did he have time for all this? How many people worked for him? The complexity of his site was quite a feat. Ghislain also wanted to be part of the world. He had no qualms sending his junk, spoiling others' lives with his need for attention. *If you no longer wish to be subscribed to this*

list, please write to readmeagain@sympatico.ca. Few people bothered to contact him. It was easier to delete the email, it was
less disagreeable for people who, like him, believed that taking action earned them special status in the world. He often
mentioned it, he'd practically founded the club. *More morons,
please! Give me another moron!* Moronity was a mental illness.
In Quebec, moronity could have been translated as *mironie*.*
Everyone would have understood immediately. *Mironie*: an illness of Quebecois literature distributors. The symptoms were
obvious: saccharine hypocrisy, confab of hatred in phantom
committees or award juries, false smiles and the contempt of
some for others, and also contempt for the entire local production in favour of the entire production of other countries
(for this symptom of the illness, see the publishing house
Les Allusifs, which found a remedy for *mironie* by publishing
translations).

—Moronity attacks the liver. At every book launch, I have a
sharp pain in my liver. My liver is so weak, I'll die of vexation.

The entire UNEQ directory, over a thousand scattered
guests, received the invite to the launch of *Prosopopoeia*. The
great spectacle of editorial speculation had begun.

Maldonne had quickly answered his prank. She wouldn't
be there; she was taking a bus to Chicago. She would complete the breathless journey from Montreal to Toronto, Toronto to Buffalo, Buffalo to Cleveland, and lastly Cleveland
to Chicago. All together, seventeen bumpy hours of shaky

---

* A reference to Gaston Miron, one of the most widely read authors of Quebec
literature, and to Jean Royer's 2004 book about Miron, called *Voyage en Mironie*.
(Trans.)

washrooms, crying babies, uncomfortable sleeping positions, bus drool on her sticky cheeks, books read, and iPod listened to until her ear canals were irritated. Maldonne was seeking a way to transform herself. No one really ever transforms, but Maldonne believed in it. No compromising the vital instinct, you need to leave when you feel you need to leave. No hard feelings, she apologized in her email, but she wouldn't write to Ghislain anymore.

Yet Ghislain knew that he had been only a transient friend for Maldonne—a listening post, activated when needed. The depressing moment when the altruistic intimacy of a friendship dies caused him a dull pain. He too would have liked to find a way to cut off ties with a strange and dying friendship.

But who is cruel enough to burn the bridges of a long friendship?

He received about twenty apology emails at most. People no longer took the time to notify you that they wouldn't be coming. Everyone was so inundated with invitations that no one bothered anymore.

The inappropriateness of his hoax matched the trouble he felt, his quiet despair. They each responded to the other. The changes in his life plunged him into melancholy.

At this moment, he would have liked to have held Courrège tightly in his arms, to have found a human being without the least trace of irony in their eyes, with whom he could have spent the evening.

* * *

LETTER TO THOMAS WHARTON
BY AN INTERPOSING NOVEL

Dear Thomas Wharton,
First of all, thank you for *Logogryph*.
Look, please try to understand me: *Prosopopoeia* is a prank in bad taste, granted. This hoax comes out of a simple Borgesian fantasy. I must tell you, however, that thanks to the success that will dissolve all our trivial preoccupations, all writers dream up such an outrageously famous book, the book of a lifetime, in their moments of indulgence. I only ask you to consider the momentary solace elicited in evoking this successful falsity, to take this unrealization into your hands and experience it. As an author, I too understand the difficult task assigned to us of creating fictional scenarios for people who haven't asked us for anything. By writing, we actually impose excess dreams, invade the fantastical ecology of strangers. Don't be alarmed by much of our violence, it's only rhetorical, an amalgam of agitation and form. Please do as I do: Forget that the ideal work does not exist and defend the fairy tale. It's all that remains.
Take care, and keep writing to us.
B. L.

10.

DIDEROT INTERLUDE

Directed by:
Stéphane Lafleur

Starring:
Rémy Girard
Pierre-Luc Brillant
Caroline Dhavernas
Chloé Bourgeois
David La Haye
&
David Lynch

COUCHE-TARD AT THE JOLIETTE METRO STOP, 10:30 P.M.
The character of Ghislain, played by Pierre-Luc Brillant, is standing behind the counter. He is waiting for customers.

A portly, middle-aged man comes in, heads straight for the jerky stand. The man, Diderot, played by Rémy Girard, then walks over to the cash register with a pack of Jack Link's beef jerky and cheddar-flavoured sticks.

DIDEROT: I am Diderot.

GHISLAIN: I am Ghislain the reader.

DIDEROT: Do you know the author of *Jacques the Fatalist?* Do you still study the book at school?

GHISLAIN: Yes, yes, I've read excerpts. It's been a while...

DIDEROT: So you know me.

GHISLAIN: By name, I know you by name, of course.

DIDEROT: You seem a bit hazy.

GHISLAIN: That's because I don't know you personally.

DIDEROT: You know me by name, like you say, but not personally. I imagine that you don't study much philosophy, do you? Do you read much?

GHISLAIN: I'm in the reading business. I work in publishing, but to pay the bills, I sell ketchup potato chips.

DIDEROT: So you also know Holland?

GHISLAIN: Yes, very well, but also by name only. But not as well as you, the Encyclopedist.

DIDEROT: They've reduced me to this, yes, but I am multiple, myriad. If I understand you correctly, they still associate me with those enlightened non-entities?

GHISLAIN: I'm afraid that's true.

At that moment, a customer, played by a very beautiful Caroline Dhavernas, comes into the dep. She walks straight to the beer fridge and returns with four cans of Kilkenny. She goes up to the till, stands behind Diderot at first, but soon gently cuts in.

CUSTOMER 1: Hi, excuse me! Could I pay right away? I'm in a bit of a hurry.

DIDEROT: Sophie?! (*Stunned, he turns around, looks at her, falls at her feet.*) Sophie. Sophie. Sophie. Sophie. Sophie. Sophie. Sophie. Sophie. Madame Volland! Did you write me back? Did you send me a letter even longer than the last one? Ah, your hands, your eyes, your belly... (*He touches the customer's stomach.*)

CUSTOMER 1 (*backing up, alarmed*): How can this guy know my name?

GHISLAIN (*cutting in*): This is Diderot. He's come to buy some beef jerky.

10. DIDEROT INTERLUDE

CUSTOMER 1: "Diderot," like my dog! (*She pays for the beer.*)

GHISLAIN: He means no harm. He's just not in the right century.

Customer 1 leaves the dep, forcibly pulling on the door behind her, but unable to slam it.

DIDEROT (*listless*): Sophie... My thoughts are my escorts, but my escorts don't think of me anymore.

GHISLAIN: I remember now, yes. I think I read you recently, monsieur. Mille et une nuits reissued you.

DIDEROT: They reissued my fairy tales?

GHISLAIN: No, cheaper books. I read *Pour une morale de l'athéisme.** It's a dialogue with a marshal...

DIDEROT: Yes, the Marshal de Broglie. But I hope that you aren't only interested in this minor work for atheists. I don't imagine this is still an issue for your civilization today, a civilization of jerky and cheddar cheese in a tube. An excellent blend of flavours, by the way. I looked into it. I'm up to date. Besides, your newspapers are terrific, and your typographers do remarkable work. You've moved on, in any case. Beyond these stupid arguments to satisfy the wizened devout and the swaggering atheists?

GHISLAIN: We ask questions to relax the spirit. We ask questions to trick our intelligence, to pass the time. To give you an example, I am nutso about ethics.

DIDEROT: "Nutso"? You eat nuts?

GHISLAIN: No, I read them.

DIDEROT: You read nutsos? Fascinating.

GHISLAIN: Of course. I'm a reader for a publishing house.

---

* *For an Ethics of Atheism.* (Trans.)

DIDEROT: In Holland?

GHISLAIN: No, here!

DIDEROT: Don't tell me that they still publish stuff in Holland.

GHISLAIN: I'm afraid they do.

DIDEROT: Ah, so you work there?

GHISLAIN: Why would I work in Holland?

DIDEROT: Good question. You tell me. And the censorship over there?

GHISLAIN: Ah, censorship doesn't exist anymore.

DIDEROT: Yes, it does.

GHISLAIN: No, it doesn't. Anyway, not here.

DIDEROT: Impossible, my dear sir. Censorship is the privilege of those who govern. Although you don't have kings anymore, you're still governed?

GHISLAIN: By a few stock market tycoons.

DIDEROT: Oh, really?

GHISLAIN: If it's an opinion, and not defamatory, we can say it.

DIDEROT: I understand: too many dead horses to beat. Freedom is the goldmine of vermin. That's not me, but an old advisor to Louis XV. But who worries about that fool now?

GHISLAIN: We punish thought crimes, but on the sly. Forced labour and capital punishment have been replaced by a series of hypocritical measures, each more degrading than the next. We live in generalized hypocrisy.

DIDEROT: If that's all, it's not all that bad. The hypocrite is harmless, sullen, an asshole. All my life, I dealt with hypocrites. They're good people incapable of doing anything well. Sometimes, they transform into cardboard fences, but their defences are easily torn down with one good kick. If that's all, you've succeeded.

GHISLAIN: Succeeded how?

DIDEROT: In the transition.

GHISLAIN: The transition to what?

DIDEROT: The transition to atheism. Bravo!

GHISLAIN: I doubt it.

DIDEROT: Why doubt it? Hypocrisy is natural. It's the fool's defence. You're not going to tell me that there are no more fools?

GHISLAIN: I'm not going to tell you that?

DIDEROT: The reason you're still working in this money souk is because you're not yet convinced that you're anything but a muzhik. I hope I'm not offending you. I'm analyzing the situation.

GHISLAIN: I've already thought about it myself.

DIDEROT: You're a serf, I will make you see it.

GHISLAIN: No one is under the obligation of anyone anymore.

DIDEROT: Yet you have accepted the rules that keep you here. Therefore, you are a vassal.

GHISLAIN: A minimum-wage employee, in any case.

DIDEROT: If I understand correctly, you have chosen your vassalage. It's ingenious.

GHISLAIN: I live through my own hypocrisy. I'm normal.

DIDEROT: You live according to the general ethics.

GHISLAIN: Exactly.

DIDEROT: Visionary books talk about two kinds of ethics: one is general, common to all nations and religions, and roughly followed; the other belongs to each nation and each religion—in this one we believe, pray in temples, advocate in our homes, and don't follow at all. So, ethically speaking, you have based yourself on the roughly general.

GHISLAIN: Yes, that's right, we're a society of the "roughly" and who complains about it, in truth?

DIDEROT: And the particular religion? Your newspapers?

GHISLAIN: Everything that's said on TV, in theatres and newspapers indicates a general movement that we more or less pretend to follow. Yes. We pray by applauding. We pray by shouting in telephonic tribunes.

DIDEROT: I love this religion of information. It's the logical continuation of the encyclopedia.

GHISLAIN (*looking at the Jack Link's pack in Diderot's hand*): Are you ready to pay?

At that moment, three people enter the dep, polite, but kind of punk: Chloé Bourgeois, David La Haye, and David Lynch. The first buys a bag of Humpty Dumpty ketchup chips; the second, a package of gummy bears, a large Oasis orange juice, and microwavable Chef Boyardee raviolis; the third grabs a twelve-pack of Molson.

Noticing that he's interfering with the smooth running of commerce, Diderot steps back to let the customers go ahead of him.

CUSTOMER 2 (*played by Chloé Bourgeois*): Are you going to the Foufs on Tuesday? (*She looks Ghislain in the eyes.*)

GHISLAIN: No, Tuesday is *Law and Order* on CTV. I'm staying in.

CUSTOMER 2: I thought I saw you hanging with the Gatineau gang.

GHISLAIN: No, that wasn't me.

CUSTOMER 3 (*played by David La Haye, in a work-family balance mode*): Don't listen to her. She's not good with faces. She's not trying to annoy you, just thinks her pet fish is a genius.

CUSTOMER 4 (*played by David Lynch disguised as a trickster, a David Suzuki of a parallel world*): Did-rot!
He addresses Diderot like they've know each other for a century. Diderot stares at him politely.
CUSTOMER 4: Did-rot! Did-rot! Did-rot! (*in broken French*) Tou est oune bonne ami de moi, a good friend. Tou est un writer de first class. Tou est oune highlight in the partition (*pronounced in English*) des loumières. But Did-rot! (*He pronounces it slowly.*) Fuck you for the mystery! Tou... We can't detruire la mystère with such force... Tou sais pas, you don't know, pas plus que toi, toi, toi (*he points at the actors waiting around him*) what hides behind the atomic tissu... derrière le soup des atomes... qui sait, who knows? (*He switches to English for the last statement.*) You should have known better, respected the power of mystery. Science is nothing but a blank sheet of paper. I'm a person who draws. I want to put the mystery back on the paper. But I'm clever, and I'm an atheist too... What do you know?
DIDEROT: I've met Benjamin Franklin. He was a perfect gentleman. I love American people. You're free of superstition, in a way. But think about that scientific sheet of paper. Everybody writes on this sheet. Everybody knows this sheet as their own. But the sheet is atomic too, and if your thinking were more subtle, you would have discovered that every sheet is a laughable symphony. At the same time, every sheet is a blank religion.
Close-up of the expressive extremities of all of the actors. Visual sequence in the hysterical kitsch style of Aronofsky's Requiem for a Dream. *Commercial exultation. The last shot lingers on the logo of Jack Link's jerky—a black bull that looks like the bear paw of Blackwater (an American private security services contractor).*

Quick superposition of the two logos, but without dramatic effect or alienating music. Then, a close-up of the door hinge; a close-up of the Couche-Tard clock indicating 10:58 p.m. Fade to black.

II.

HERACLITUS MOTOR HOME

WE ALL RESEMBLE BOOKS THAT NEVER END AT THE right page.

Ninety-nine percent of books are from the past. There are no more steps when the end comes *ad nauseaum*. Let's stop there. Ghislain. Ghislain. A two-cent character in a cheap comedy. Come back, turn around, rewind your monkey's street organ, your word machine.

Nothing ever ends. Everything transforms. Memory doesn't give rise to anything anymore. Ghislain talks to himself. Ghislain agrees with the third person singular. Ghislain has returned to singularity. Nothing left except robots of the self, clever ordinary creatures, voices adjusted for showrooms.

Ghislain saw nothing, knew nothing. He's sobering up in

the tunnel of dead hours. The mercantile tunnel of change: Heraclitus motor home.

Make no mistake: Ghislain is drawn from life. He breakfasts early and leaves, sobering up because he has to, his head back in his bed.

Ghislain can't manage to think for himself at this moment, so he delegates.

He delegates while sitting in the book's antechamber. The sliding door opens onto thwarted ambitions.

All around him, the narrowing of his focus redefines the world. It's an endless thread of spongy polymer, soft and empty inside.

The end no longer has any reason to be in a world where the impossible no longer holds.

Ghislain spits, drinks some water, rises in his bed from the beginning. Nothing ever ends, no cause, no consequence.

Ghislain would like to cry, because that's the stuff of fiction. All this noise for nothing, all life to improve the fate of the species.

Hitting the woods, beating the hog, running towards destiny.*

Ghislain coordinates his end while delirious about Malcomm Hudd. It's his choice. He stuffs you in a waxed bag and puts the lot over a fire, in a double boiler. Boil quickly for two minutes. Set on a chaste porcelain plate; knead with the stomach; knead with the eyes; knead with your most significant past.

---

* A nod to Raymond Queneau's 1980 book, *Courir les rues, Battre la campagne, Fendre les flots* (Hitting the Streets, Mounting a Campaign, Making Waves). (Trans.)

Ghislain is not dead; Ghislain does not dream; Ghislain is not in agony; Ghislain has decided to delegate everything because it suddenly weighs on him to repeat himself, to admit in front of the mirror that even lies don't amuse him anymore.

Ghislain thinks about Maldonne, who pretends to be resting on a bus on her way to Chicago, and it does him good to smile thinking about this bitch who believes in the relocation of thought, and to whom he is attached, almost aggressively, through confusing emotions.

Maldonne talks to Ghislain in her head on the bus that's towing life along at a steady speed. She removes her earphones. Wonders what she's doing there, suspended in the weightlessness of delicious comfort. Then goes back to her reading.

Maldonne is reading. No one sees the title of the book she's reading. Everyone knows that reading alone makes you seem suspicious, disrespectful, or treacherous. If you read, you die less than me; if you read, I need to be on guard. We need to pray for those who read. No idea is guaranteed; no author. Maldonne is heading towards her freedom in a straight line.

Maldonne dog-ears a page, underlines a few lines. Each time she takes notes, she looks out the window at the world flashing by in a Warholian long take.

Twelve hours of this, three hours of that, six hours of this, eight hours of that, so much time to kill between two headaches and two unexpected conversations with the stranger on duty.

Chicago will be her cure. Chicago will be where she'll shed her skin. A cicada's dry exoskeleton on a moist blade of grass.

Pleasure doesn't stop anything, and books make us cough,

redirect our instincts for the worst, also for the better. So much the worse.

The bus lulls the passengers to sleep in the tribal night of the Great Lakes, forest roads, and myriad mythologies. Books on strange trees, on menacing seasons. Books on nocturnal monsters.

Maldonne sees the faint light of a PlayStation screen in a child's hands, his eyes full of concentration. He's also reading. This child is reading the world, and she doesn't understand it better than him, she who contemplates.

We live among local scenes and characters, among the hyperintelligent of the technological city and the trash-picking kids of São Paulo.

We are all mirrors. We understand so little of what surrounds us that we start to conceive, invent games to soothe the spirit.

The darkness changes shape beyond the windows.

The darkness clarifies the world, accentuates the echoes.

We advance without knowing the end. Holding it within us, because we have yet to arrive there.

Acknowledgements

Thank you to Elyssa Porlier for her invaluable help with my research in the field (Couche-Tard). I would also like to thank my translator, Oana Avasilichioaei, for her excellent work—a tour de force—and for maintaining the richness and elegance of the English language, while composing with the book's numerous changes of register. Lastly, I wish to thank J. C. Sutcliffe for mentioning that *Lectodôme* (*Readopolis*) had yet to be translated in a review of *Universal Bureau of Copyrights*—my first English translation (also by Avasilichioaei)—published in the *Times Literary Supplement*. His mention helped put in motion the process that lead to this translation. In this respect, I also wish to salute all those who helped make *Readopolis* a reality: Éric de Larochellière, the publisher of Le Quartanier; Jay and Hazel Millar and the BookThug team. —B. L.

Thank you to Ingrid Pam Dick for being *Readopolis*'s first reader. I am deeply grateful for her sharp mind, wise council, and crucial suggestions. —O. A.

Bertrand Laverdure is a poet, novelist, and the current Poet Laureate for Montreal (2015–17). A prolific writer, Laverdure is the author of three books of poetry and four novels, including *Lectodôme* (2008), *Bureau universel des copyrights* (2011; published in English by BookThug as *Universal Bureau of Copyrights* in 2014), and *La chambre Neptune* (2016). He has won many awards for his work, including the 2003 Grand Prix du Festival International de Poésie de Trois-Rivières, and the 2009 Grand Prix littéraire Archambault for *Lectodôme*.

Montreal-based poet, translator, and performer **Oana Avasilichioaei** has published five poetry collections, including *Expeditions of a Chimæra* (with Erín Moure, 2009), *We, Beasts* (2012; winner of the A.M. Klein Prize for Poetry from the Quebec Writers' Federation) and *Limbinal* (2015). Previous translations include Bertrand Laverdure's *Universal Bureau of Copyrights* (2014; shortlisted for the 2015 ReLit Awards), Suzanne Leblanc's *The Thought House of Philippa* (co-translated with Ingrid Pam Dick; 2015), and Daniel Canty's *Wigrum* (2013).

Colophon

Distributed in Canada by the Literary Press Group:
www.lpg.ca

Distributed in the United States by Small Press Distribution:
www.spdbooks.org

Shop online at www.bookthug.ca

Designed by Malcolm Sutton
Copy edited by Ruth Zuchter

BOOK
PRODUCTION
WAR ECONOMY
STANDARD